THE UNLIKELY MESSENGER

William McFadden

First Edition, July 2019

ISBN: 978-0-578-51853-4

Printed by: IngramSpark
www.ingramspark.com

For any inquiries regarding this book, please contact the author at
https://williammcfadden.blogspot.com

Cover Design: Trevor McFadden
https://sites.google.com/view/conte

I dedicate this book to the Lord Jesus Christ. May Your glory shine through. To my wife, thank you for your big help with this and believing in me. I will always appreciate it. To my older son, thank you for the cover art and the additional help. May you grow as an artist in your own right. To my younger son and my daughter. You are special and loved by God. To the loving memory of my grandmother, who encouraged me to write books, and may you rest in the arms of the Lord Jesus Christ. Finally, to any who have medical conditions and disabilities. You are loved and prized by God.

FOREWORD

The Scriptures used in this book are mostly from the World English Bible (WEB). Other translations were used as appropriate.

If one wants to nitpick at some error at what some character says, it's intentional. Stories, whether true or that of fiction, are made up of imperfect and fallible people. If we have perfect, infallible people, then we don't have much of a story. And it would be quite a bore in my humble opinion.

The aim of this book is to show everyone is made in God's image. Genesis 1 has radical truth. If one took this truth that all humans are made in God's image seriously, then it would totally vanquish any attempts to dehumanize others.

Thank you for choosing to read this book. I appreciate it. Hope you enjoy the story. May moral and just people stay prominent in our society and protect those who can't protect themselves or protect those who are marginalized. May we never use social safety nets as a means to dehumanize or extinguish the life of others.

1

LET'S SAVE HIM

"A hermaphrodite!"

"You mean...intersexual."

"Whatever."

Two doctors looked on a naked man unconscious. His wrists were slashed.

"What happened?" asked the second doctor.

"Apparently, 'he'," responded the first doctor as he used air quotes, "was found in his bathtub passed out with the water running. Neighbors complained of water constantly running. And water flowed out his apartment till the landlord got in. Anyway, it looks like this guy wanted to off himself."

"How do you know that?"

"He overdosed on drugs and slashed his wrists."

The second doctor looked down at the man for about thirty seconds. She felt compassion for the hermaphrodite. And then she looked up at her male colleague. She felt frustration at his unwillingness to help.

"Let's save him."

"Why? 'He'," the first doctor used air quotes again, "obviously wanted to kill himself, so let him die. We—"

"You know what? I am getting tired of those air quotes. Stop it."

She looked at him sternly. The other doctor shook his head.

"We can't afford to take care of people who want to end their lives."

"It's not law yet," she countered, "so let's stop arguing and start helping him before he dies."

"Can you blame him for wanting to kill himself?" asked the doctor as he motioned his hands at the unconscious man. "Look at him. He's a freak. We don't treat Undesirables."

Just then, the woman doctor slapped her male counterpart.

"No, he's not. He's made in the image of God!"

The male doctor put his hand over the cheek she slapped. He looked at her in amazement.

"What are you, some kind of Christian?"

"Yes, yes, I am," admitted the woman. "And I will pay for his care, the law allows me to treat 'Undesirables'," she said in air quotes.

"So, let's save his life now."

2

LEAVE ME ALONE

Sam woke up in a hospital bed. He looked around and found himself in a recovery room. There were two other beds: one on his left and one on his right, but they were empty. The only source of light was from the outside. He could see what time of day it was. It appeared to be late afternoon. Gray clouds covered the sky. From what he could tell, it was raining.

He pulled the blanket down to his waist. He saw that his wrists were bandaged. He was angry.

"You jerk! You are not going to let me die, are you," he said as he looked up. "We'll see about that."

He was about to pull off the bandages when a woman walked in. She was in her late thirties to early forties and was somewhat thin but not emaciated. She wore a black turtleneck with brown dress pants. She had shoulder-length, wavy golden-brown hair. Her skin had a slight bronze hue to it. She possessed a natural beauty that did not necessitate much in the way of cosmetics.

"Hi," said the woman.

Sam did not respond. He stopped what he was doing and just looked at her. When he noticed that she was holding a Bible, he became annoyed.

"How are you feeling?" asked the woman.

"What do you want," demanded Sam.

"I just wanted to see how you're doing," the woman replied somewhat sheepishly. "It was touch and go for a bit there, as I was told."

"Why do you care?! Who are you anyway?"

"Well," responded the woman calmly. "I'm a chaplain." She slowly came towards Sam.

"I care because God cares about you. I was wondering if you needed someone to talk to or pray with, or maybe I can read something from God's Word." She placed the Bible on his bed.

"Get the hell out of here! And take this crap with you," he said as he threw the Bible against the door.

"I HATE God! You know why."

"Why?"

"Because of this," said Sam as he pulled off the blanket and lifted his gown.

The chaplain stood there. She started to cry.

"Yeah, you know what else. I burn down churches and vandalize them. And I attack born again a-holes like you. But since you're a very attractive gal, I don't want to harm you. So, get the hell out of here. Now!"

The chaplain headed towards the door. She opened the door. She paused and she turned around.

"You know, just remember that Jesus loves you and because He loves you, I love you too."

"Leave Jesus out of this. It's his old man I have a problem with. Now leave."

The chaplain left. Sam started crying. He cried till he let himself hear the rain falling outside. The rain soothed his soul and helped him go to sleep.

3

AN UNLIKELY ENCOUNTER

An orderly bot opened the door of Sam's room. Sam was still asleep. The rainfall intensified outside. The bot went around tiding up the room. The bot saw the Bible after cleaning up the room. It picked the Bible up and placed it on Sam's lap. Sam covered himself with the blanket. The robot then proceeded to take out the trash and quietly left the room.

The gentle rain morphed into a tempest. The hospital doors were sealed. It also levitated about ten feet off the ground, as required, to avoid possible flooding. The generator sustained the hospital's power and the lives of its patients. But most of the hospital was dark to conserve power. Sam's room was mostly dark except for a small light above the door. The wind and the rain buffeted the window.

Sam woke up. He sat up. Sam looked around the room to find out what the noise was. He remembered it was raining. Sam was amazed at the strength of the storm. He felt something on his lap. He looked. It was the Bible.

"It's probably that cute but annoying Bible thumper," he said to himself. "Well, this thing is going in the trash."

But something caught his eye that made him stop. He noticed the Bible was opened. He picked it up. Despite the small source of light, he could see what was written. The words piqued a curiosity. Sam reasoned to know his Enemy more. So, Sam skimmed through 2 Corinthians 12 till something in the text captivated his attention.

"...there was given to me a thorn in the flesh, a messenger of Satan to torment me, that I should not be exalted excessively. Concerning this thing, I begged the Lord three times that it might depart from me. He has said to me, 'My grace is sufficient for you, for my power is made perfect in weakness.' Most gladly therefore I will rather glory in my weaknesses, that the power of Christ may rest on me. Therefore, I take pleasure in weaknesses, in injuries, in necessities, in persecutions, in distresses, for Christ's sake. For when I am weak, then am I strong."

The Scripture puzzled Sam. How could this follower of Christ be delighted in following if his suffering wasn't taken away? He looked at the beginning of the 2 Corinthians and found out it was a man called the Apostle Paul who wrote this. Sam pondered what the messenger of Satan and thorn in the flesh meant.

Thunder roared nearby. Sam became angry after thinking about it. He looked up in a sneer.

"If this is true, you are a cruel master, you know that. You made Paul suffer and you made me like this. That's why I want nothing to do with you! You make me sick!"

The thunder roared again after he launched his indictment at the Divine. This time the thunder was above the hospital. Sam shuddered. For the first time, a fear of God entered Sam's heart. The already turbulent wind and rain pounded the window even harder. Sam got nervous. He wondered if the window would break. The hospital swayed significantly in the storm. But, the levitation system seemed to tether the hospital to the ground. The wind got stronger and the levitation system had to be cranked to full power. The technicians were hoping the storm would die down soon because the system can't sustain this all night. To avoid panic, they didn't tell anyone, though.

Sam's heart raced, and his palms felt clammy. Sam felt the Bible slip from his sweaty grip. But, he held onto the Word of God. Sam reread the passage. In the midst of the storm, some words in this passage began to allay Sam's fear.

"My grace is sufficient for you..."

Sam pondered this. The more he thought about it, the more Sam felt. Could God be graceful, even when someone is in turmoil? Thoughts swirled around in Sam's head.

Lightning flashed outside the window. Thunder roared again. Sam felt weak and insignificant. But he reread what Paul wrote.

"For when I am weak, then am I strong."

"This is stupid," Sam protested. "Why am I falling for this? It's nonsense."

Sam leapt up to throw away the Bible, but he was too weak to stand. He fell to the floor and the Bible flew from his hands. Sam managed to lift himself to a crawl. The Bible was a short distance from him. He crawled toward it. Each crawl was a struggle.

"I AM going to throw YOU away if it's the last thing I do."

He grasped the Bible. The Scriptures flopped opened at Acts 9. Sam stalled again to dispose of the Bible. The rain continued to hammer down on the hospital. The small light above the door flickered for a few moments. The hospital wobbled while the light flickered. Stability and power returned, and Sam was yet again drawn into what he read.

Sam read that Saul was threatening the church and went to the high priest to get letters to capture men and women who followed the Way as it was called. Sam immersed himself in the story. He became Saul. In an angry zeal, Sam rushed forward towards Damascus. I must rid the world of these troublemakers and their lies, Sam thought.

Sam's lungs burned and ached, sweat beads poured over his eyes, his breathing was rapid and shallow, the muscles in his legs strained, but the desire to fulfill his holy mission to rid the earth of these vicious vermin overrode any feelings of pain and discomfort. They must be stopped, Sam thought as he dashed towards Damascus.

He ran with such force and speed; the others who were with him struggled to keep up with Sam. He could see Damascus ahead. Sam smiled. I will destroy, yes, I will destroy, he mused. It became his mantra as he plowed towards the city.

A blinding light from the sky suddenly appeared. It burned Sam's eyes. He fell.

"Ahhh!" screamed Sam. He was prostrate with his eyes closed and his arms flailing around. His hands searched in vain to grab onto something.

"Saul, Saul," said a voice from heaven.

"Sam, Sam," said a voice.

Sam immediately stopped what he read and looked around the room. He didn't see anyone. He shook his head and started reading again.

"Why do you persecute me?"

"Who are you Lord?" Saul asked. Sam became briefly detached from Saul since he thought he heard his name called out.

"Sam, Sam," said the voice again.

Sam looked around the room. The rain, wind, and thunder did not relent in their fury.

"Hello? Is there anyone here?"

No answer. Sam's heart started to race a little again. He looked around again and waited for a response. Nothing. So, he went back to reading the story.

The Lord said, "I am Jesus, whom you are persecuting. But rise up, and enter into the city, and you will be told what you must do."

Sam read that the men who were with Saul heard something but didn't see anything. Saul couldn't see anyone after his encounter with Jesus. So, they led him by the hand to Damascus.

"Sam, Sam," called the voice again.

Sam threw the Bible across the room.

"That's enough! Show yourself."

No one responded. Lightning flashed outside the window. Thunder bellowed. It shook the window. Sam could hear some patients in the distance scream in fear.

"Show yourself, now!"

Sam looked up. "Is it You?"

"Then, show Yourself! I have many bones to pick with You. Come on, man up and face me."

Lightning hit the hospital. A thunder more ferocious than before roared above. The hospital's levitation system was failing. It rocked violently. People screamed. The technicians were trying to keep the hospital from falling. Sam slid against a wall in his room.

"Ahhhh!" Sam cried. He tried to get up but couldn't. Someone's right arm reached down and grabbed Sam's hand. Whoever helped him up had incredible strength. Sam rose up quickly. The other arm was over Sam's shoulders. He felt something peculiar about this person's hand. A flash of lightning reaffirmed his thoughts. It had scarred indentations in the palm of the hand. The person helped Sam back to his bed. The storm was still furious but seemed to subside a bit.

Sam saw who helped him. He shook in fear. Sam's eyes grew wide. His lips quaked and his teeth chattered. He couldn't utter a sound. Sam's breathing became rapid and shallow. The person was a bearded man, Middle Eastern in appearance. His beard was salt and pepper along with His longish hair. The man had a slight muscular build. His eyes seemed to be emblazed with fire. His gaze pierced Sam's soul. His countenance was authoritative but warm. He had a golden crown that gleamed and jeweled of too many colors to count. It created an ethereal light among the darkness. He wore a majestic robe that was white, yet most of it was dipped in scarlet. He wore a golden sash around His chest.

"Ar—Ar—Are you?"

"Yes, Sam, I AM," responded the Man in a deep but friendly voice. This was the same voice that called Sam earlier.

"Sam, Sam, don't do this to yourself," said Jesus as He moved closer to Sam. Jesus held Sam's hand and looked into his eyes again.

"I love you."

At that moment, Sam seemed to be transported to elsewhere. He was in the midst of a crowd. Sam and the others were looking at three men on a small hill. They were hanging on huge wooden crosses. The people hurled insults at them, especially at Jesus, who was in the middle.

Sam didn't realize it was Jesus at first, because He was so disfigured and bloody from a result of a severe beating. This Man was wearing what looked like a crown of thorns on His head. It looked like this crown was shoved on Jesus's head. The thorns pierced His scalp and forehead. Streams of blood ran down His face.

"He saved others, now let's see if He can save Himself," declared some in the crowd. "Let Him come off that cross, so we can believe He's the Son of God."

"Yeah, let's see," shouted others. Even the other men hanging on the crosses insulted Jesus.

Sam realized this Man was Jesus. He looked very different from His royal demeanor.

"Father," gasped Jesus, "forgive them for they don't know what they are doing."

Sam suddenly found himself in his bed with Jesus at his bedside.

"Do you understand how much I love you." Jesus's scarred hands held Sam's. Sam didn't respond to the question. Sam wasn't sure of anything anymore. Was he delusional or was he actually talking to the King of kings, as Jesus's followers call Him?

"You do what you don't understand." Jesus let go of Sam's hands and looked up at him again. Jesus touched the side of Sam's face. Sam felt Jesus's scar on his cheek. He never felt so much love and care from anyone before. He was an outcast. If Sam had been born a few years later, he would have been terminated in his mother's womb.

Undesirables, or anyone with physical and mental abnormalities, are terminated by law before they are born because society can't afford to care for them. They were too many bodies to care for and too many mouths to feed. These Undesirables, as they were called, received minimal care, if any. Job opportunities were scarce for them. People already could barely survive.

They needed jobs more than these blights on the human collective. So many Undesirables were destitute. Sam was fortunate enough to have a job.

Tears fell from Sam's eyes. He put his hand on Jesus's. Sam held onto Jesus's hand tightly. If this was a delusion, then let me indulge in it, Sam reasoned. But if this is real, then even better. But what now, Sam thought, what now. He continued to look into the flaming eyes of the Creator of the Cosmos.

"You have zeal and passion for what you think is right and wrong," said Jesus. "But zeal without knowledge isn't good." Jesus closed His eyes and shook His head. "For now on, you will have zeal for Me and My Kingdom. You will have passion for My ways. Follow me, Sam. Trust me. Obey me. Love me. I love you, Sam. I will always be with you if you follow me."

Lightning flashed across the sky again, followed by thunder, and Jesus vanished.

"Okay, Lord. Okay," Sam cried. He wiped away the tears of joy admiration for his King.

"I love you, Sam," said Jesus's voice.

"I love you too." Sam feel asleep with a peace he never felt before. The storm dissipated shortly after.

4

TIMID BEGINNINGS

The next morning, the chaplain timidly entered Sam's room. She went to retrieve the Bible. She wanted to give it to someone who would be more receptive. Few would ask for prayer these days. Even fewer would ask for a reading of the Holy Scriptures or request a Bible. Most of the time, the chaplain would sit there and listen to the patients' testimonies of pain and suffering. She would offer encouragement to them and offer to pray with them. But, she had to very careful not to break any Religious Moderation laws. She didn't want any complaints of proselytizing. Half of the time, the chaplain wondered why she was here in the hospital.

She saw Sam reading the Bible. When he read it, Sam had puzzled looks at times. Sam didn't notice her opening the door. The chaplain stood there for a few minutes just watching him read.

She meekly went towards Sam. She almost tiptoed towards him.

"That...was some...storm we had last night," she stammered.

"Yes. Yes, it was," replied Sam with his eyes on the Bible. He read for about a minute more and looked up. He saw it was the chaplain. He smiled at her. The chaplain noted something was different about him. What it was she couldn't tell.

"Well, I was here to take the Bible—if you're not interested," she said in a meek tone. She was looking down at the ground as she said this.

"No, don't bother."

"Re—ally, it's okay," she responded, looking up at Sam again.

"No, I want to keep it. I want to learn about Jesus."

The chaplain had a puzzled look. Then she asked a question.

"What changed your mind?"

Sam kept smiling and his eyes grew wide.

"I have seen the Lord."

"Oh," responded the chaplain. She nodded. "That's great." She was still puzzled. "Well, the Bible does show us...."

"No, you don't understand.... I HAVE seen the Lord!" Sam exclaimed with both his hands spread out and moved with every word he spoke. "Listen ... uhh... what's your name?"

"Beverly."

"Sam."

They shook hands.

"He was HERE in this room, Beverly. He came during the violent storm. I cursed God and was going to throw away the Bible. I fell down. But Jesus helped me back up into the bed. He knew my name. He was dressed in a white royal robe dyed in scarlet. He wore a golden sash. He had a magnificent crown with the jewels that illuminated this room when it was dark. He showed me when He died on the cross. I saw the scars on His hands." Sam pointed to his palm of his right hand. He spoke with intense emotion and almost in a booming voice.

"I felt His scars, Beverly. I felt His scars." Sam touched the side of his face and rubbed it. "He touched my face." Tears streamed down Sam's face. "I have never felt such love ever."

Beverly stood there. She didn't know what to say. She started crying too. Beverly wipe away tears and sniffed.

"You know what Jesus said to me?"

"What," Beverly asked as she continue to cry.

"He said He loved me. He told me that my zeal and passion will now be used for Him and His Kingdom. Jesus told me to follow Him. Who is He, Beverly? He's a King. I want to know Him. I have either lost my mind or Jesus actually came to me in this room. I don't know what to think or where to go with it. All I know is that Jesus loves me, and I love Him too."

"I—I—don't know what to say, Sam."

Beverly paced around the room a bit. "Wow! I still don't know what to say." She came back towards Sam's bedside.

"You're going to help me, Beverly, find out who He is," he grabbed her arm as he pleaded. Beverly was shocked. Her fear of Sam gave way to compassion. She looked into Sam's eyes. She could see in his eyes he was lost in a sea of helplessness, but he had a compass of hope. "Beverly, I want to know Him, *please.*"

"Okay, I will help you," Beverly agreed. She nodded. Beverly hugged Sam tightly. "I will help you. And you will help me too." They cried for a while.

- 13 -

5

AHA...I CAUGHT YOU

"Aha!"

Beverly and Sam turned around. It was the male doctor who didn't want to treat Sam. The door was opened behind him. A layer of smugness plastered over his face. He crossed his arms, slowly tapped his left foot, and shook his head.

"Beverly Bonnevera, you have violated a no proselytizing code in the Religious Moderation Acts. Not to mention inappropriate touching of the patients. Oh, girl, I will report you!"

"I was waiting for you to trip up someday," the doctor spoke again. "And now, aha, I caught you!"

"NO, I have caught you," rebuked a voice behind him. It was the woman doctor, the one who used her money to save Sam.

The first doctor spun in a swift one-eighty motion. His smugness evaporated to reveal fear.

"I have heard of you sneaking up on conversations between spiritual counselors and patients and reporting on them, but I can never prove it till now."

The doctor remained speechless. The other doctor was chief of staff.

"So, Dr. Jones, you are violating the privacy laws between counselors and patients. And you may be committing fraud, since it's the patient who needs to report if their rights are violated under the Religious Moderation Acts."

"I also noted," continued the chief of staff as she paced around the room a bit, "that you lost what's important about being a doctor: helping people. Your performance is horrible, and you treat patients like they're a nuisance. I have seen in your records you do nothing or next to nothing for even simple care. Yes, our societal health system is overwhelmed and tottering, but let the politicians figure it out. In the meantime, our jobs as doctors is to help people the best way we know how, even if it's risky for our jobs, regardless what murky policy is in place. People first. You are not just here to collect a paycheck."

Dr. Jones' fear subsided for a moment. He had a gleam in his eye. He had one more card to play.

"Jean, I will report you for possible sedition, giving religious preferential treatment, and wasting resources," he said shaking his finger. "I don't care if you are the chief of staff. You will lose your position."

Jean remained stone-faced.

"Go ahead, Ted. Go ahead. Report me. We will have a hearing anyway. In the meantime, you are suspended till further notice."

Ted walked up to Jean till he was inches from her face. He scowled.

"Make me leave, Jean. When I'm done with you, I will regain my rightful place as chief of staff. And you will be competing against janitorial bots for a job."

"Leave now!"

"You and what army," Ted said as he shoved Jean.

Sam and Beverly just sat there and observed. They didn't know what to do.

Jean was unfazed by the shove. She moved her head to face the hallway. Jean motioned her head for someone to come in. Two police officers with heavily armored suits came in. They wore helmets that had violet tinted visors covering their eyes. They were heavily armed. One of them shook his head and signaled Ted to leave the room with his index and middle fingers. Ted complied.

As Ted and the officers were leaving, he turned around.

"I'm not done with you, Jean! You hear. This isn't over!"

Jean remained in the room till the officers and Ted left the hallway. Jean looked at Sam and Beverly and smiled.

"Be careful Beverly. And, God bless you, Sam. I am glad you are alive."
She left.

6

HAUNTS NEED NOT APPLY

"In a 450 to 250 vote, the United Gaia Council has passed the Life Enhancement Act," the voice reported from the TV screen in Sam's room. "This will give people, especially Undesirables, the right to terminate their life at any time. The Act is expected to be approved by the President General today or tomorrow."

Sam just watched the TV.

"The government expects that this will greatly alleviate the strain on the healthcare and social systems. Undesirables, born before the Genetic Sustainability Act, which mandated to terminate anyone who had physical or mental abnormalities, have been clogging the courts with lawsuits for access to healthcare and jobs. They now have the opportunity to easily terminate themselves. Here's what someone who's suffering has to say."

The screen shifted to a man with cerebral palsy. He looked emaciated and haggard. His clothes were tattered, and his eyes were black and hallowed out.

"Thank you, UGC, for allowing me to end my life peacefully," he said in a grateful but resigned voice. "I don't have to fight anymore." He started crying.

The anchor reappeared on the TV.

"The law will further reduce the overload of the system since those over sixty-five can now die peacefully. Care will now be restricted to a minimum when one becomes this age."

The anchor continued in praise over the law.

"This act will dovetail with the reinforcement of the Healthy Population Act. This will restrict families to a size of four. Those over that size will again face penalties."

The TV flashed over to a politician. He was a middle-aged, black haired, bearded Caucasian man who wore glasses. His hair receded in the front slightly. A reporter asked him a question.

"How will these acts benefit the healthcare and social programs?"

The politician coughed and pushed his glasses back on the bridge of his nose with his middle finger.

"You see we are giving people who are ineligible for care and other benefits the freedom to alleviate their suffering. Thereby...", he coughed again. "Thereby, reducing or eliminating the legal challenges in our courts. This will save the people money and provide more benefits and aid to others who need it. And by the reinforcement the Healthy Population Act, we can give our society an incentive to sustain Mother Gaia by having a reasonable population. Natural resources will be alleviated. Global climate as well as overall ecology will improve because of sustainability. We can ensure our survival for generations to come by this regulation. Not to mention, our healthcare will be even more sustainable, less need for more urban expansion, and our social safety nets will be less stressed. Education and employment will be sustainable. So, these acts are a win-win for everyone."

The TV flashed to the anchor. "However, not everyone agrees."

The screen showed a crowd protesting in front of what look like a government building. The crowd was diverse. Some held up signs that "All people are made in the image of God" and read passages of the Bible as well as praying and singing to God: "You are good, all the time, You are good." Others were reading the other religious texts like the Quran and the Torah. Anarchists were also dressed in black trench coats that had a white peace symbol in the front and a white anarchist Circle A in the back. They held signs that said, "Dehumanization is the end of liberty" and "End the war on humanity." There were also families and those who were advocates for Undesirables. They were chanting and holding signs that said, "Undesirables are people too."

A female reporter commented as the screen showed the resisters, "Protestors have lined up in front of the capitol building."

The screen flashed to a man yelling on a megaphone. His face was concealed in a black mask with a light blue pattern all over it. The pattern resembled something between a grid and a Rorschach blot. He also wore a grey long brimmed hat. The man was slightly stocky and spoke in an accent from a place once known as Texas. He was known as the Janitor for his constant exposes on government and corporate corruption and abuses. He would jam signals to get his messages out. The Janitor would also leave drop files of his reports in random places.

"We have let the New World Order conquer the planet. And now, they are launching their extermination program on humanity. They are picking easy targets like 'Undesirables' or the elderly or bigger families. But the New World Order won't stop till they reduce population to their liking. So, what's next: color of skin or eyes or where you're from. Perhaps, what religion you believe. In any case, we can't let us slide further into darkness and tyranny. We must stand our ground and reclaim the world for liberty and humanity!"

"Yeah," roared many in the crowd. "Stand our ground! Stand our ground!" They chanted a little more but quieted down.

Beverly entered the room quietly as Sam was watching. Sam acknowledged her. She just stood and watched the drama unfolding in the front of the capitol.

Police in heavily armored suits guarded the building. They had the same helmet with violet visors as the ones who escorted Ted out of here. Sam could see the insignia of the earth on the shoulders of the suits. They wielded shields and shock lances. The police stood in a phalanx position.

"Clear out of here," a voice ordered from the side of the police. "You are blocking government officials from leaving."

The crowd didn't comply. Someone started chanting, "Stand our ground, stand our ground!" More in the crowd picked up the rallying call.

Beverly and Sam watched in nervousness. The tension between police and protestors was so taut, Sam and Beverly wondered when it would snap. Their answer may have come. Another crowd came towards the protestors. It was a counter-protest.

"You Haunts need to shut up and go away," said a man who seemed to be leading the counter-protest. He looked Caucasian but had a bronze tinge to him. He was surprisingly well-dressed for a gathering such as this. "You Haunts are obstacles to our survival and progress. Mother Gaia can't sustain us much longer this way."

The others in the counter-protest started chanting.

"Haunts, Haunts go away! Go find somewhere else to pray!"

They repeated this mantra at the haunts. The protestors were trapped in a pincer attack between the police and the counter-protestors. The second crowd started shoving the first. A few were pushed into the shock lances. The first group of protestors started to push back.

"No, don't push back," shouted the Janitor. "This is what they want. We must show the world how corrupt and tyrannical this system is. We must be willing to take the abuse while standing our ground!"

Some counter-protestors attacked the protesters.

"Can't stop! Won't Stop! Killing people is quite enough," shouted the surrounded protestors. They continued to repeat this even they were pushed on the ground and beaten.

The violence got worse as some people wearing black masks and black trench coats came rushing toward police. They had red anarchist symbols on their backs. They suddenly emerge among the protestors. They also attacked the counter-protestors.

"No, stop them," pleaded the Janitor. "These are provocateurs!"

These masked provocateurs threw Molotov cocktails at the police.

Whether what the Janitor said was true, no one knew. Sam did see the squad leader of the police turned to another officer and nodded. The other officer seemed to be pressing something on his lance.

The police phalanx charged into the anarchists and protestors. Then, robots descended onto the crowds and sprayed gas on them. Pandemonium broke out.

"Ahhhh!!"

Everyone, except for police, were choking on gas. The screen got cloudy and the transmission stopped.

7
IMMERSED

Sam felt a pit in his stomach about the future. But the shroud of fear dissipated as Sam remembered what the Lord Jesus told him. Sam's Lord valued him and that's all that mattered. Sam was thankful for living, now certain he was going to use this second chance at life for God, whatever that may be.

Beverly turned towards Sam. She held his hand.

"I'm sorry. I will do everything I can to make sure you are okay."

Sam shook his hand. He let go of Beverly's hand.

"It's okay. I know that Jesus and God value me and that's all that counts now. Whatever happens, I just have to take one day at a time."

Beverly nodded and she pulled out her Bible.

"A part of following Jesus is that you are baptized or immersed to show your commitment to Him. Let me read what Jesus says."

She flipped to the place she wanted to read.

"Jesus came to them and spoke to them, saying, 'All authority has been given to me in heaven and on earth. Go and make disciples of all nations, baptizing them in the name of the Father and of the Son and of the Holy Spirit, teaching them to observe all things that I commanded you. Behold, I am with you always, even to the end of the age.' Amen."

Beverly closed the Bible and put it down on Sam's bed. She tucked some hair behind her left ear that had fallen in front of her face.

"Now since Jesus has ultimate authority, He ordered His disciples to make others into disciples too by teaching them to obey Him. A part of obeying our Lord is showing others you have died to your old life and are now living Christ's way."

Beverly pulled up a chair and sat by Sam's side. She grabbed the Bible to open it again.

"Or do you not know that all we who were baptized into Christ Jesus were baptized into his death? We were buried therefore with him through baptism to death, that just like Christ was raised from the dead through the glory of the Father, so we also might walk in newness of life. For if we have become united with him in the likeness of his death, we will also be part of his resurrection; knowing this, that our old man was crucified with him, that the body of sin might be done away with, so that we would no longer be in bondage to sin. For he who has died has been freed from sin. But if we died with Christ, we believe that we will also live with him; knowing that Christ, being raised from the dead, dies no more. Death no more has dominion over him. For the death that he died, he died to sin one time; but the life that he lives, he lives to God. In the same way, consider yourselves dead to sin, but alive to God in Christ Jesus."

Beverly closed the Bible and looked up at Sam.

"So you see, it's like we die to sin like when Jesus died on the cross, and we raise up again in a new life like Him too. We are supposed to be imitators of our Teacher and God."

Sam was a bit puzzled about this. He rubbed his cheek and chin for a minute to ponder the meaning of baptism or immersion.

"So, Beverly, how does someone get baptized then?"

"Well, ideally, I believe when you confess that Jesus is Lord and God raised from the dead, you should be completely submerged in water and you come up after going on. From my understanding, I believe the word 'baptize' means to completely immerse yourself in water. But, other brothers and sisters see it differently. So, if it's not possible, you can sprinkle or pour water over you. The point is that you make a profession of faith in Jesus Christ and show others your confession by getting baptized. So, if you're interested, you can wait till you get out of hospital or I can baptize you now in front of others."

Sam nodded his head.

"Well, I see what you're saying about completely immersing yourself, but I want to obey my loving Lord and Savior, so please baptize me now."

"Okay," Beverly replied. She got up and opened the door to leave. Beverly returned about an hour later. Two people walked in. It was a man and a woman. The man shook Sam's hand.

"Hello, my name is George."

The woman waved at Sam and shook his hand.

"Hi, my name is Nadine."

Beverly also called for Jean to come to the room as well. Everyone just waited for a few minutes till Jean came. Beverly nodded at Jean and then turned to face the others.

"According to the Religious Moderation Acts, I must ask the person who is converting to a faith if they are doing this without coercion. And I must have an official present to witness this person's free choice. Dr. Jean Talara," said Beverly as she turned to her again, "you are the presiding official in this person's conversion?"

"Yes, I affirm I am the presiding official," replied Jean in a clinical tone.

"Okay, great."

"Now, Sam Lysander," Beverly said as she faced him, "you have expressed an interest in converting to Christianity. Is this so?"

Beverly sighed after she said this government speak. Sam nodded and responded.

"Absolutely! I will follow Jesus, my Lord, wherever He goes."

Sam was adamant about his confession. He couldn't deny what he experienced: Sam either lost his mind or Jesus really appeared to him. But, Sam felt having an official present to approve of something sacred was intrusive and ridiculous. But, Sam didn't dwell on this thought much further.

"Okay," Beverly responded. "I have George and Nadine here to witness your baptism into Jesus, not because it's required, but because we Christians live in a spiritual community together. We are here to help each other out and it can be lonely at first, so I brought these two to see if you want to connect with them."

"No offense to George and Nadine, but what if I wanted to speak with you instead?"

Beverly felt awkward towards Sam's request, especially when he made remarks on how pretty she looked. She never had anyone ask this before. Beverly felt called to be chaplain, but she always tried to keep it professional. She referred patients to other people and groups but never asked nor recommended anyone to have a spiritual or personal relationship with her. Other than going to church with Nadine and George at times, she lived a lonely life. She felt it was better this way after committing to the Lord Jesus Christ. But when she looked at Sam, she had compassion on him and put her aloofness to the side.

"Well, umm...okay. That's fine. We can do that. You should be getting out of here tomorrow," she said as she looked at Jean to confirm this. Jean nodded to affirm what Beverly said. "I'll come by tomorrow and discuss when we can meet up about the Bible or any other spiritual matters."

Beverly cleared her throat. She went to the sink and filled up a pitcher that was sitting nearby. She came back towards Sam and the others. She was about a few feet from them.

"Stand up, Sam, and please come over if you can."

After some effort, Sam got out of his bed. He was a little wobbly but able to make it. George and Nadine helped him along the way. Sam stood in front of Beverly. Beverly held the pitcher. She and Sam looked at each other in the eyes. She smiled. He smiled back.

"Sam Lysander, based on your firm profession of faith—and may you continue in the Lord Jesus Christ for the rest of your days no matter what—I baptize you in the name of the Father, the Son, and the Holy Spirit."

Beverly poured water over Sam. Sam closed his eyes as she poured. When the water covered him, Sam felt something that no words could explain. He felt clean, new, and empowered. His soul was at peace for the first time ever. He felt the same feeling when he saw Jesus.

"Sam," a voice called in his mind. "You now have my Spirit like all those who truly follow me. In time, you will proclaim my name everywhere and suffer for it, but I will be with you."

When Beverly finished pouring the water, Sam opened his eyes. His demeanor seemed different.

"Jesus has all authority in heaven and on earth. He sits at the right hand of His Father. He has granted freedom. But all creation must bow to Him," Sam declared loudly.

8

NOW WHAT

Sam looked down on his wrists. The deep slashes were not there thanks to Jean paying to regenerate his skin. Otherwise, he would have been lucky if he got bandages. Sam then looked up to thank God for saving his life.

Sam wanted to quit his job as a chemist at the narco shop. It troubled his soul to keep working there. He knew that drugs were harmful to others. And, he couldn't make money off of people's misery anymore for he cared about others now. But when he got to the narco-shop, they told him he didn't have a job anymore because they thought he was dead. The official record stated Sam Lysander died due to suicide. They hired someone else. Sam wondered how long it would say he's deceased before it got corrected.

Sam ended up in front of his apartment. He placed his thumb on the bio-lock to open the door. The bio-lock scanned his thumbprint, but it rejected Sam. Sam tried again. It rejected him again. He tried again, still rejected. He wiped his thumb on his shirt, hoping to clear the dirt, if any, on his thumb. Sam tried, but the bio-lock still said no. Sam tried his other thumb and the bio-lock rejected him again. The bio-lock told Sam to see the landlord and warned if he tries again, the police or police bots will come.

Sam went to the landlord's apartment. He knocked on the door. No answer. Sam knocked again but this time a little louder. Still no answer. He pounded on the door.

"All right, I'm coming!" yelled the landlord from the inside. Sam heard him thumping towards the door. The door opened. The landlord was bewildered.

"You—you—you're alive, kid?!"

The landlord was a middle-aged, tall heavyset fellow, who had a somewhat muscular build. He had a bronze complexion, black shoulder-length frizzy hair, thick black eyebrows, and a mustache. The landlord's bushy chest hair crawled out of his white tank top. His yellow and brown striped boxers partially covered his thick muscular, hairy legs, which looked like massive trees in a forest. Sam saw the landlord's enormous belly hanging out of his shirt. The cigar in his mouth and the beer bottle in his hand slipped out the same time when he saw Sam.

Sam got a similar reaction from those at the narco-shop, when they dropped the drugs or paraphernalia, with faces turning white, as if they have seen a ghost or someone raising from the dead. But in a sense, they were correct with their reactions. Sam did raise from the dead, spiritually.

Fortunately, the bottle didn't break. Beer kept spilling out on the plush leopard print carpet till it could spill no more. Its yeasty smell ascended between Sam and the landlord. The cigar rolled outside at Sam's feet. A gentle breeze caused its wispy smoke and fragrance to waft upward as well.

Two women came out from the kitchen to see what the commotion was about. They were the landlord's wives. They were wide-eyed in disbelief. One put her hand on the shoulder of the other and whispered something. The other confirmed what she heard. The first wife seemed be asking a question. The second wife then turned to look at the first and shrugged.

"It's okay, ladies," said the landlord after he quickly turned to look at them. "I got this." He motioned them with his eyes and bushy brows to go somewhere else. They scurried away. He turned back to Sam. He put on his stoic veneer that he had towards the tenants.

"What can I help you with?"

The landlord asked this in a shallow manner for he almost knew what Sam would say next.

"Well, I can't open my door because it no longer recognizes my thumbprint."

The landlord nodded his head in more of an affirmation of what he thought Sam would say, rather just nodding in understanding Sam's plea for help.

"So, what do you want me to do, kid?"

"Can you help me get in?"

The landlord shook his head. "Sorry, kid. I can't do that."

"Why not?"

"I thought you were dead, so I cleared out your apartment, repaired the water damage from your attempted suicide, and gave the apartment to someone else. I can't have an empty apartment, that's the law. You were dead, at least I thought so, and your apartment became fair game. Sorry, my hands are tied. Can't help you."

The landlord was about to close the door, but Sam stopped him.

"Wait, what about my stuff? Where is it?"

The landlord sighed. "It's probably in the trash and recycling. You can check there. Maybe it's there. Maybe it's not. Wouldn't be surprised if someone took it or the sanitation bots already got everything out. Sorry, kid. Good luck." He closed the door and a laser gate covered it.

Sam went to the trash and recycling area. He looked around for a while. He couldn't find anything except for a few items and a couple of changes of clothes, but they were filthy and moldy now. Then, a light beam scanned his face.

"Warning, unauthorized presence," declared an electronic voice. It was a police bot that the landlord hired as security. It descended just a few feet away from Sam. It was armed with electro-cannons and Gatling guns. It was also armored.

"You are to leave immediately. You have 60 seconds before consequences will occur."

Sam dropped whatever he found and left.

"Thank you for your compliance. Have a good night." The police bot hovered in the air to make sure Sam left.

Sam walked some ways down the street. He looked up to God.

"Now what? Where do I go from here?"

Sam began to cry.

Then, a car pulled up by Sam.

"Sam," said a familiar female voice.

Sam turned toward the car. He wiped away his tears. It was Beverly.

"What's wrong?"

"Everything. I have no job. No home. Because everyone thinks I'm dead."

"You're not, Sam. You're not. God has made you more alive than ever. You will see."

"What am I supposed to do, Beverly? I'm lost."

"Trust the Lord Jesus. Now get in the car. You can stay with me."

She nodded and the door opened. Sam was hesitant at first but got in.

"We'll take this one day at a time, Sam. You, me, and God. We'll figure how to help you."

Beverly and Sam drove off.

9

HMM...

Beverly parked the car. They both got out at the same time. She walked towards an alleyway. Sam followed. Beverly stopped and put her hand on the side of a building in the alley. A black, metallic box suddenly materialized and was floating in front of her. She took her phone off her ear and put it in the box. The box vanished. Cloaking technology. All forms of it were banned after the last global war when the world formed the United Gaia Council. Of course, it was rumored the government still used this technology despite the law.

Sam noticed Beverly used an external electronic device, whereas most people opted to put in neuroputers.

"Don't ask," Beverly said. "And if you want to be free, I would suggest taking that off."

She pointed to the implanted device on the side of Sam's head behind his right ear—his neuroputer. Technology was one of the few pleasures that Sam enjoyed in life. Society marginalized him, but technology didn't care.

Sam didn't think about his machine. It was like his hand or foot. Just a part of life. He tried using it a couple of times after his attempted suicide, but it didn't seem to work. But the content he consumed and saved on his machine maybe wasn't pleasing to God.

Sam didn't say anything.

"Look, I can save all the information on your machine and transfer it on another external device I have. The point is that you shouldn't be tracked and watched every moment."

Sam's stomach felt sick. Everything he viewed, enjoyed, experienced has been watched and recorded by others.

"No, Beverly! There's no need to save anything. Get rid of it and destroy it."

"Are you sure?"

He nodded. Beverly pulled out a retractable knife. It looked sharp and menacing. She quickly sliced out the machine. Sam felt a bad pain and warmth for a moment, but it was gone.

"It's okay, I had put a skin patch on you."

Beverly stabbed the device and smashed it. Sam felt behind his ear. It was as if it was never there. He felt a burden come off. He felt free. It was like the feeling he had when he met Jesus. Though Beverly had a skin patch, which only medical professionals should have, he didn't question it. Maybe chaplains could have it. Who knows, he thought. He was grateful anyway.

He followed Beverly down the alley. She kept going till she stopped in front of a door of a small brick building. The door was unusual. It was wooden and it had locks with keyholes. She used a key to open her door. Sam had read and seen pictures about old style doors and keys, but never actually seen them. They were relics of the past.

When Sam entered Beverly's home, he saw more relics. He saw books on a bookshelf. Beverly noticed Sam looking at the books. Other than Bibles he either burned in the past or what Beverly brought in the hospital, he never seen actual books in his life.

"Good ahead, Sam. It's fine. They're just books."

Sam, with some hesitation at first, went over to the bookshelf. It was full. He saw a few Bibles, including the one Beverly brought to the hospital. There were other works by authors he never heard of before, such as CS Lewis, Chesterton, Tolkien, PKD, and Ursula Le Guin. One book caught Sam's eye particularly. He slowly pulled it off the shelf. It was called "The Cost of Discipleship" by Dietrich Bonhoeffer. It had a cover of Jesus sitting on a mountainside speaking and a disciple sitting on a rock below Him listening. Sam handled the book in awe. He slowly turned a few pages and read what was inside.

"Now that is a great book," Beverly said with her index finger up and moving as she spoke. "You can definitely feel free to borrow or take the book."

Sam read a paragraph or two more and carefully slid it back into the bookshelf. Sam looked around. Beverly's house seemed somewhat Spartan. Other than the bookshelf in the living room, there was a wooden chair pushed against a small round table. In the kitchen, there was small wooden square table with four rickety chairs. He also noticed a hallway that led to two bedrooms and a bathroom probably.

"If you need to use the bathroom, it's down the hall to the right," Beverly affirmed what he thought. "There's also a guest room there where you can stay till we figure what to do."

"Thank you, Bev," Sam said.

"It's Beverly," replied Beverly. Beverly hated being called Bev.

"Sorry. I'm just a little nervous."

"It's okay." she said softly. She smiled at Sam.

Beverly walked over to the kitchen and pulled out of the pantry a small bag made of burlap. She put it down on the counter. She washed her hands. She took a pot and filled it with water. She turned on the stove and put the pot on it. Sam just stood in the living room watching the whole thing.

Like the books, it was rare to see anyone cook like this anymore. Most either didn't cook and got packaged food from the mega-corporations and government, or you used machines to cook your food if you had money. Others, like Sam, would sometimes pick fruits from any trees they could find. Sam thought that many things Beverly was doing today were odd and unique. This was an intriguing dimension to the chaplain. Beverly turned her head toward Sam.

"You want some natural-made pasta? It's way better than the junk that comes from the likes of Dragon Corp."

After the water came to the boil, she opened the burlap sack and poured pasta into the pot.

"Yes, thank you."

She pulled out another gunny sack from the pantry. This one caught Sam's eye. It had a black and white Circle A symbol on it. Is Beverly an anarchist?

Anarchists were considered dangerous by the UGC, but there was no real evidence to back that claim up. Anarchists, at least the ones Sam were aware of, either lived in communities and cooperatives or lived by themselves. They traded freely with each other and would freely help each other too.

Every time supposed anarchists committed violence, all known anarchists would denounce and say these are provocateurs from corporations or the government. And they provided legal defense to those accused of violence by the government. Fortunately, they would win most of the time. One thing that others knew for certain: many anarchists took care of their own. This very fact is what attracted many people to anarchism.

Anarchists would set up shop in cities at times, but they would get pushed out shortly after by local governments because they miss some esoteric regulation somewhere, or the corporations who didn't like getting undercut or outperformed. Both the government and the corporations were especially brutal to those anarchists who tried to help in times of crisis.

Beverly turned around to Sam. She grinned at him.

"Why don't you come closer to see what it's in the sack."

Sam came towards her. He looked down. It was coffee beans. The aroma from the beans delighted his nose.

"I buy from anarchists because they get a far bigger share from their fruits of their labor than those who are under mega-corporations. As a follower of Christ, I must show my love towards others in every way possible, including what I purchase. It's all God's anyway. So, brother, you want any coffee?"

"I sure do."

She grinded the beans. She filled up a small pot with water to put it on the stove. The pasta was done. She made it al dente. Beverly drained the pasta of water. She then took some meat strips made of lamb, beef, and chicken. It was meat that came from an anarchist cooperative. Beverly fried them in a pan. When they were done, she chopped them into smaller pieces. She sprinkled the meat all over the pasta, mix the two around, and finally drizzled the dish with olive oil.

She then took the boiling water from the smaller pot and poured it into a glass carafe. Beverly took the coffee grounds and put them over two metal cone-shaped coffee filters, which rested over two cups. Beverly slowly and intermittently poured the water from the carafe into the coffee filters till she was done. When the water completely flowed through the filters, she removed them and dumped the grounds into a small can.

Sam was amazed how fast Beverly did everything. The aromas from the pasta dish and coffee were the best things he ever smelled. Beverly got two plates and put the pasta on them. She placed them on the table. Silverware and napkins were there already. She also placed a bottle of blackberry and pomegranate seltzer on the table along with glasses. Beverly put them down shortly after she boiled the water the second time.

"Come and eat, Sam."

Sam pulled out the chair for Beverly. Beverly smiled.

"Thank you."

"It's the least I can do after you have gone through all this trouble for me."

"It's no trouble at all."

Sam sat down in his chair. Beverly thanked God for the meal. She then lifted her glass.

"Here's to our Lord. May He reign forever."

"Amen," Sam replied. They clanked glasses and started to eat and drink.

10

PAST WOUNDS

Smash! The coffee cup crashed to the ground. Coffee splattered everywhere. Sam acted like he'd seen a ghost.

"Sam, are you all right?!"

He said nothing. His eyes were wide, and his mouth ajar. Sam's lips quivered. Tears rolled down his cheeks.

Beverly got up toward Sam. She tried to put her hands onto Sam's arms, but he pulled away. He turned away from her.

"What is it? Talk to me."

"No, I can't!"

He still wouldn't look at her.

"Please."

"No!"

"Sam, come on. What's wrong?"

She gently placed her hand on Sam's shoulder. He still wouldn't look at her.

"You don't understand, Beverly. It will change everything."

"Sam, I don't understand. Tell me. Please."

Sam cried for a bit. He sniffed and wiped away his tears. Sam gently pushed Beverly's hand away from his shoulder. He nodded.

"Okay, I'll tell you."

He turned to face Beverly.

"Beverly, I did this to you."

"What did you do? I don't understand."

He softly touched her neck. Beverly had a wide scar that went from her right side of her neck to the top of her left breast. Sam just touched the neck area. Sam never saw this past wound till now.

"Beverly, I tried to kill you."

He cried. He buried his face in his hands. He cried out again.

Beverly was stunned. Sam continued to cry. After about a minute, Beverly spoke.

"Sam, I—I don't know what to say."

Beverly looked down to collect her thoughts. Sam stopped crying and looked at her. She looked him in the eye. Beverly didn't seem angry, just confused and a little scared. A thought crept into Beverly's mind—was Sam here to finish her off. She took a couple of steps back, but no further. She felt if she tried to run, then Sam would try to catch her or attack. Sam knew if he went towards Beverly, then it would just make her run or fight.

"Beverly, I need to tell you what I did and why I did it."

"Uhh...okay. But do we need to re-live what happened? Can we drop it?"

"Beverly, I don't know if I can."

Beverly closed the door of the church building behind her. The building was old and needed repair. It was a slow day at the church. No one showed up for counseling or whatever they needed for a few weeks. When she preached, only a few rows of pews were filled on Sundays. And it continued to dwindle.

She felt the crisp, night air of early Autumn touch her face. She closed her eyes to enjoy the zephyr flowing through her hair. She took a deep breath. When she exhaled, she opened her eyes. The breeze was only a fleeting comfort. She wrapped her scarf around her neck and walked down the small staircase in the front of the church building. She stepped onto the sidewalk.

Beverly saw a hovercycle zooming down the street. It flew down the road in a fury heading towards her. She froze in fear. The rider looked like a raging specter. It had a long raven black hooded cloak with iridescent highlights. It was flying from the speed. The apparition had a fiery red skeletal face. The demon howled as it drew a long razor sickle from his sheath. The blade gleamed in the moonlight. The Grim Reaper, Beverly thought. But couldn't run because she was paralyzed in fear.

"Die witch! Go to hell! Ha, ha, ha, ha!"

The Angel of Death sliced right through Beverly. Blood flew. She didn't feel the pain immediately. It happened so fast. She flew back from the force and bounced on one of the walls of the decrepit church building. Fortunately, she missed the stained-glass window by a few feet. She fell back on the street. Her head gashed open, but her skull didn't break. The ghostly attacker threw a bomb at the front door. It exploded. Flames engulfed the building. The rider vanished into the distance, howling and laughing.

"God, help me," pleaded Beverly. She passed out.

❧

"From that moment on, I couldn't shake it off," said Sam.

They were standing in the kitchen. Beverly stayed where she was at as he recounted what happened that night.

"Whenever I vandalize churches or hurt Christians after that, your face kept showing up. Your look of horror as I...I sliced into you."

Tears welled up and fell from his face.

"It ate away at me more and more till I wanted to kill myself."

Sam sobbed and cried. Beverly slowly stepped towards Sam. She put her hand on the side of his face.

"Sam, it was a very traumatic night. I thought I was going to die. But, that tragedy turned my life around. And God used you to save me."

Sam was bewildered. Beverly continued to have her hand on his cheek. She looked him in the eyes.

"I was a hypocrite. I was playing games with God. My life didn't honor Him. I didn't believe that the Bible was God's Word. And that Jesus was the Word of God that became flesh. I had as the Scriptures say, 'a form of godliness but denying its power.' Though I preached from the Bible, I treated it as tradition and folklore with grains of truth, rather than honoring it as God's truth. I lead people, in the flock God entrusted to me, astray with my attitude and unbelief. Rather taking what God said at face value, I believed the machinations of men."

Tears rolled down her face. Beverly started to sob too.

"But that all changed that night. When you hurt me, I called out to the God of the Universe. As...as...I lied on the ground in pain and bleeding, I pleaded to the only One who can help me. He saved my life; He saved me from my sin. From that moment on, I couldn't shake off the fact God is real, and the Lord Jesus is more alive than ever. The Spirit is more real than each breath I take. So please, please Sam don't let this guilt hold you down."

She came closer to him till she was just inches from his face. Tears still flowed from both Sam and Beverly.

"You may have meant it for evil, but God used it for good. I forgive you. I love you."

"Thank you," Sam said. "But I don't deserve your forgiveness."

"Nobody does, Sam. It's called grace. It's not earned but given. If God has forgiven me of my sin, and He has sent His Son to pay for all sins, no matter how evil, what right do I have to withhold forgiveness from you? Please let us put this behind us and never talk about it again."

They cried some more and embraced each other.

11

SMILE...

"Come to me, all you who labor and are heavily burdened, and I will give you rest. Take my yoke upon you, and learn from me, for I am gentle and humble in heart; and you will find rest for your souls. For my yoke is easy, and my burden is light."

Sam looked up after he read Jesus's words. It reaffirmed the freedom he had in Christ.

"Before I surrendered to the Lord Jesus, I was in bondage to how society acted, my physical condition, and my sins. But it all changed when I met Jesus."

Sam was speaking before a group of people. He told them about his life before and how Christ had freed him. Sam was standing behind an old, rickety wooden pulpit. The group of people, young, old, somewhere in between, had something in common: their love for Jesus Christ. They were inside a gothic style church building.

Christians, these days, would either meet in homes or in decaying cathedrals. These architectural artifacts may look dead on the outside, but life was vibrant on the inside. Their spirit was far from extinguished, but they weren't sure what to do.

What was peculiar about the zeitgeist among Christ's bride was the word "Christian" nearly fell out of vogue. They would call themselves as "Christ-followers", "lovers of Jesus," or "faithful subjects to King Jesus, "or the like. The Church recognized the word Christian became meaningless or became way off base of who Jesus was.

Sam moved in with George now. Beverly and Sam still met up, but it wasn't as often. George helped Sam learn the Scriptures. Sam devoured the words of God. It became his passion to learn more and be more like Jesus.

Sam left the pulpit and sat back down. The other believers clapped and some shouted "Amen."

"Thank you for sharing, brother Sam," said a woman who approached the pulpit. "Anyone else?"

Beverly stood up and went to the podium.

"Hello, everyone."

"Hi," responded several.

She opened her Bible.

"As they went on the way, a certain man said to him, 'I want to follow you wherever you go, Lord.' Jesus said to him, 'The foxes have holes, and the birds of the sky have nests, but the Son of Man has no place to lay his head.' He said to another, 'Follow me!' But he said, 'Lord, allow me first to go and bury my father.' But Jesus said to him, 'Leave the dead to bury their own dead, but you go and announce God's Kingdom.' Another also said, 'I want to follow you, Lord, but first allow me to say good-bye to those who are at my house.' But Jesus said to him, 'No one, having put his hand to the plow, and looking back, is fit for God's Kingdom.' "

Beverly closed her Bible.

"I had lived a life of unbelief and sin. I liked our Lord. I was attracted to His teachings like 'love your neighbor' and I preached that to the congregation I once had. But like these people, I wasn't willing to completely commit myself to Him. And I led others astray by not telling them this important truth. Following Jesus, or as some of us still call it Christianity, is about submitting completely to Jesus Christ. Nothing more, nothing less."

"Preach it," someone said.

"God sent His Son to break down that wall between us and Himself. Jesus tore down that curtain on the cross. Death couldn't hold Jesus in that tomb. Now, our King reigns, and someday He will return and restore it all."

"Amen," the congregation shouted.

"But unfortunately, I denied this essential truth about Jesus Christ to others. Their lives suffer for it, as well as mine until I was on a sidewalk nearly dead."

Sam squirmed a bit. Though the guilt dissipated, he was uncomfortable hearing it. He knew Beverly was just telling her testimony. She wasn't trying to rehash old wounds.

"And I cried out to God! Our God corrected me of my rebellion and saved me from my sin. I was carrying a heavy yoke, but as Sam pointed out, Jesus has a light yoke for us.

She met Sam's eyes. She smiled at him and blinked her eyes slowly. He smiled at Beverly. The feeling of discomfort disappeared.

"He took that old heavy burden of sin and gave me His light yoke of freedom. All I had to do was to respond to His call to humanity: 'Follow me.' "

She left the pulpit and sat back down. People clapped.

"Thank you, sister Beverly," said the same woman.

"Now, brother George will give us his lesson."

George, who was sitting next to Sam, approached the pulpit.

"Thank you everyone for sharing your testimony as well as reading from the Word. What everyone has said dovetails to what I'm about to talk about."

He opened his Bible.

"Therefore if anyone is in Christ, he is a new creation. The old things have passed away. Behold, all things have become new."

George looked up.

"Before God changed our hearts, we were lifeless and empty like the world was before He breathed life into it. We don't see life the same way anymore—through the lenses of narcissism. We see life through the eyes of the Holy Spirit. He guides us to be like Jesus, our King, who serves to please our Father in Heaven. We live to please God. That is our new way of life. And when our Lord Jesus returns, all will be made new. Now what do we do in the meantime? Do we still just sit around to wait for Him to return?"

George had started calm but got more and more passionate as he spoke. Then, George paused and looked up a little further than normal. He looked at the camera bot looking at him and the congregation. It was there every time they met. It was a part of Religious Moderation Acts. Everyone was free to practice what they believed, but they couldn't take things too far. And to ensure this, either police, bots, or drones would patrol the houses of worship. But those who totally acquiesced to the regulations weren't subject to these watches that much.

The camera bot looked like a metallic spider about three or four feet big. It discreetly crawled around in the upper parts of the walls and the ceiling. It's red and violet lenses zoomed and retracted as needed. It was the analyzing the situation, trying to determine whether this congregation was cause for it to strike or not. On its thorax, it had a symbol of the scarlet ten-headed dragon. The emblem of Dragon Corp.

This spider could have been smaller if it weren't two constraints. One, lawsuits had forced these spy machines to be big enough for people to see.

They were small, almost nano-sized before. Two, the effects of the last worldwide war put technology at an almost standstill. Advanced technology was blamed for mass destruction. Many things that were invented before the war were now banned.

"Are we going to contain our hope and the foretaste of the new heavens and new earth to this forsaken mausoleum?"

He kept his eyes on the camera bot. The robotic spider eyed George too. The robot just stood there. George was silent. He gulped. Nadine, who also sat next to Sam, Sam, and a few others also noticed what George was doing.

It was like a spiritual standoff between George and the machine. The camera bot wouldn't back down, but would George?

He looked down at the congregation. Most now noticed what was going on. He saw little ones holding their parents. The mothers and some fathers held their babies. Some in the congregation looked puzzled. Others were scared from his silence. George heard a murmur among them. He saw people whispering to each other, followed by shrugs. He saw the older ones and the Undesirables. They looked vulnerable.

He looked up at the camera bot. Its cold, piercing stare remained. George wanted to do everything he could to protect the flock, but he knew he must honor the Lord Jesus Christ no matter what. He gulped again. He looked back down.

Nadine and Sam just nodded for support.

"We must," he said in a meek voice. "We must show this in our lives, so that others can see the light of Christ and love of God."

Nadine stood up and clapped. Sam followed. Everyone else did too. George bowed his head. He walked away from the pulpit with his head down and red-faced. He didn't sit back down by Nadine and Sam. He took off in the back somewhere. The camera bot just watched and eventually moved on to something else.

12

HE KNOWS OUR FRAME

George ran into a backroom of the church. It was used as a storage closet. He pushed over a box on a rack. He punched the part of the wall where the box covered. George punched a hole through the wall and quickly pulled out a gun. It was a military issued weapon from the last global war. People weren't allowed to arm themselves, except for some puny peashooters and small, cheap knives. But, the government and the bodyguards of the mega-corporate elite had total liberty with arms, even though all military forces and weaponry was abolished. Anyone cynical would say law enforcement was just the military in police clothing.

The gun was hidden, as others have done with banned weapons. They only come out in case it was needed. George sobbed. He put the gun to the side of his head.

"Noooo!!"

Bang!!

Nadine, Sam, and Beverly were stunned. Nadine was the one who screamed. George collapsed. The gun slid out of his hand. Nadine dashed over to him. She sobbed loudly and almost hyperventilated after a couple of minutes. She clasped his body. Her hands were on his bloody hair.

"Nooo!! Why?! Why?!"

She started hitting him. George surprisingly was still breathing but it was very shallow. His pulse was weak and fading fast.

"We were going to start a life. You would be my husband. I would be your wife. Why did you do this to me?!"

Beverly ran to her side and consoled her. Nadine still held George in her lap. She stopped hitting him.

Sam stood where he was. He could see twitches in George's limbs. He noticed George's lips slightly quivering. It looked like he was trying to say something but couldn't. George's eyes were closed. Tears rolled down his cheeks.

Nadine saw his lips trying to say something. She put her ear toward his lips to hear what he was saying. But, she couldn't.

"Please come back to me. Noo—oohh—noo—oohh!"

Sam kneeled to pray. He cried.

"Father," he said in a weeping voice. "I know all things are possible. You raised Your Son from the dead. Lord, You also raised the dead when you were on earth, and You used Your apostles to raise the dead at times. God, I pray and I plead for You to heal my brother. We are not to take our lives because You bought us with a price. But Father, You know our frame and we are dust. Your love and mercy endure forever. Please don't hold this act against George. Lord, we are powerless to do anything, but You are powerful. May Your will be done."

Sam knelt in silence. Nadine and Beverly huddled together. Both cried. George's lips and limbs stopped moving. His breathing stopped and pulse disappeared. Nadine cried over George's body. Sam sobbed.

Beverly noticed some from the congregation stood in the room too. Crying and shaking their heads in pity and compassion. They were starting to go over to try to get George's body from Nadine.

"No," protested Sam. "Leave them be."

Sam got up. He felt the Holy Spirit guiding him towards Nadine, Beverly, and George. He knelt by them and put his hands over George's bloodied head. Blood drooped over George's face. Beverly and Nadine had a puzzled look. Sam raised his head upward with his eyes closed.

"In the name of the Lord Jesus Christ, please raise up this man!"

About a minute went by. George started breathing again. His pulse returned. He opened his eyes and looked at Nadine. George began to speak.

"I am so sorry! I shouldn't have left you like that."

He was crying. George's speech was slurred but comprehensible.

"I don't blame you if you want leave."

Nadine said nothing. She just kissed him. She held him in her arms. She shook her head.

"I would never leave you, my love. I want to be your wife."

"Praise God!" some exclaimed.

"Yes, praise the Lord. It's all Him," Sam responded. "It's all Him and His power."

Beverly went over to Sam and hugged him. Sam put his arms around Beverly as well.

Weeks went by since that day happened. George was nowhere to be found around the church.

Beverly took over preaching and teaching while George remained at home. Beverly didn't hold the gatherings at the old church building. She would meet in homes to preach and teach, or whatever place she could get away from the all-seeing eye of the State. When she would gather the entire congregation together, it was in a small patch of woods outside the city. She didn't like the aerobots patrolling the city skies. They would go back and forth into a ship called a sentry that remained hovered over the skies with an ever-watchful eye over the denizens.

George sat in his chair. He was at home with Sam. He was recovering quickly. He was able to walk again. The slurs disappeared from his speech for the most part. He continued to improve each day. But, mentally and spiritually, he needed to heal. George sulked around the house. He was withdrawn. Nadine would come by to visit him, but it didn't lift his spirits. He didn't talk to Sam. Sam left him alone. He figured he would give George some space.

George's face was unshaven. He stayed in the same clothes for a few days. He was just staring at the wall while sitting in the chair.

Sam opened the front door. Sam came home after having lunch with Beverly. He saw George just sitting there in his unkempt condition. Sam was about to pass by to his room, but he decided to sit across from George. He couldn't remain silent anymore.

"Hey, George. How's your day?"

George said nothing. He just kept staring at the wall. The only response Sam got was the rocking noise from George's chair. The rocking chair was wooden. George inherited the rocking chair from his grandfather. Sam just heard the rocking.

"George ... George."

Sam got up from his seat. He stopped George from rocking.

"Hey, man, come on."

George turned his head slowly toward Sam. He gave Sam a blank stare.

"You can't keep this up, George."

"Yes. I can," replied George.

Sam was somewhat amazed that George spoke. It was very clear.

"I feel like such as a hypocrite, coward, and failure."

"You're none of those things," Sam replied.

"Really?! Really, Sam."

Sam seen some life come back into George, but it was full of anger and frustration.

"I balked in the front of the camera bot! I then go try and kill myself. I disappointed God and Nadine. Do I need to make myself more clear?!"

Sam said nothing. George continued to speak. He got up.

"I couldn't take that constant surveillance anymore. That robot constantly monitoring what I say. I'm tired of tempering my words and being worried that if I say anything that's deemed radical, there will be consequences."

George paced around the room. Sam hadn't seen George moved from the chair for a while. If it weren't for this venting, Sam would've been happy for him.

"Sam, I can't let them shut down our congregation. That old church building is all we have. It's decaying and falling apart, but it's all we got. I have to protect this local cell of the Body in every way."

George put his hand over one of his eyes and slid his hand back a bit over his forehand and his hair. He started to cry.

"We're....we're just hanging on till Jesus returns. We can't do anything. This world is too far gone. And I don't know why God saved me. And Nadine....I broke her heart. I—"

"That's enough, George! Do you think you're the one who guards this congregation?!"

Sam grabbed George by the shoulders.

"So what. We lose that old dusty mausoleum of a building? That's nothing. You think some stupid law is going to stop God's will?!"

George said nothing. He just gave Sam the same blank stare he gave earlier.

"Jesus has all authority in heaven and earth, and nothing, not even these camera bots, can stop Him or His Kingdom. You are expecting far beyond what God expects. It's not about saying the 'right' words. It's about taking your stand in the Lord Jesus Christ and following His Spirit. We can't change the world, but God can."

George pushed Sam away.

"I'm a failure to God, to Nadine, and to everyone else."

"You're a failure by sulking around and staying in a despair. You're playing into Satan's hands right now."

George said nothing.

George slapped Sam.

"Shut up! What the hell do you know?!"

Sam held the cheek that was slapped. Sam's nose bled. Rivers of emotions flooded into Sam's mind. He felt the rush of anger where he wanted to pummel George. He also felt a deluge of sadness that drown the anger. Sam wanted to run. He felt hot tears wanting to pour out. But, Sam resisted his urges. He stood firm and turned the other cheek.

"I do know this, George," Sam answered. "Like a father has compassion on His children, so Yahweh has compassion on those who fear Him. For He knows how we are made. He remembers that we are dust. But with God are all things are possible."

He walked past George and left the house.

13

CROSSING PATHS AND BLADES

Sam walked some ways. He ended up in front of the old church building. A gang of Nihils stood in front of it. Sam went up the stairs to go inside, but they stopped him.

"Hey, hater! You're not going anywhere."

Nihils were like a hybrid between goths from past eras and phony punk skinhead types. They were adherents to nihilism. Some Nihils also held to transhumanism and would modify their bodies with robotic implants. The one in front of Sam amputated his left arm and replaced it with a robotic arm. He also replaced his right eye with a red optic. He wore a black trench coat. He was a burly fellow. The other Nihils fall behind him. He seemed to be the leader.

"Please let me through. I don't want to cause any trouble."

The leader shook his head. He gave a cold grin.

"I'm sorry. We're not going to let you through that easily. You see your kind already caused trouble. You acted all kind to the people of this community, but you use this as a cover to spread your hate and oppression."

"Please let me through. If you need credits, please take."

Sam pulled out his wallet. He tapped it and credits appeared.

"It's not much, but please take it all."

The Nihils laughed.

"We're not here for your money, moron! But since you offered, we'll take it."

One of the Nihils swiped the wallet out of Sam's hand. He gave it to the leader.

"We're here to send you a message to stop your poison. You will not keep humanity in darkness."

The leader pushed Sam hard. Sam almost fell. The Nihils surrounded Sam. He wasn't sure what to do.

"Lord, help," pleaded Sam.

"There ain't nobody who's going to save you. Where's your god now?! Ha, ha, ha!"

Then, the leader threw a punch from his robotic arm toward Sam. Suddenly, a razor-sharp blade whizzed through the air. It dived down with a fury at the leader's robotic hand, piercing it. He couldn't land a punch at Sam.

"What the—!"

"Back off!"

The Nihils and Sam looked up. They saw a figure, dressed in black, standing at the top of the old church building. The black clothing looked like armor of some kind. There were a few throwing knives, along with flash bombs strapped to the armor. Old tech, but effective. The figure wore an armored black mask. It looked like the mystery person couldn't see or breathe. But that wasn't the case. From the voice and the appearance, this was a woman.

"Hey!" yelled the leader as he pulled out the blade from his hand. "Why don't you come down and fight me!"

"Yeah, come down and fight us," jeered the others.

The Nihils forgotten their rage against Sam. They redirected it toward this shadowy enemy.

"Are you sure you want that," the mystery woman replied, calmly. "I don't think you'd like it."

"Let's see. Have at you!"

The woman descended deftly down the church building. She was in front of them.

"Stand aside," said the leader to Sam. He pushed Sam away.

One of the Nihils threw him a small metal bar. He caught it with his robotic arm. Everyone heard a metallic whoosh. A huge, menacing axe appeared in his hand.

"Eeeeeyahhh!"

The leader charged towards the woman. She just stood there. Sam was mortified at what was about to happen. The leader got close to her, but the woman smoothly dodged the attack. He crashed into the front door. It broke off from the frame. The axe made a giant gash into the oak door, but it got stuck. He rammed against the butt of the axe. His face bled a little from the crash.

He pulled the axe out. He turned around.

"You just got lucky. Now, die!"

He charged at her again. This time, he lifted the axe with both hands above his head. She ducked and pushed up a bit with her back against his chest. He flipped over and rolled down the stairs and landed on his back.

"Aaaghh!! Get her!"

The Nihils rushed her. She flipped over them. They crashed into the wall by the smashed door.

The leader staggered to get up.

"What's wrong with you morons?! After her!"

The Nihils, still somewhat dazed and confused, went after her again. She rolled aside. They toppled over onto their leader, who was still sprawled out on the stairs.

"Ahhhh!" screamed the leader as he got dogpiled.

Sam chuckled at the whole thing. He felt bad after, but he couldn't help it.

The leader burst through the pile. The other Nihils flew in different directions.

"If you want something done right, you need to do it yourself!"

He held his axe, looked upward, and roared. He leapt to the top of the stairs.

"Get back," said the mystery woman to Sam.

He ran towards at her full force. He leapt into the air. As he jumped, he swung the axe in a diagonal motion. She was about move back but there something wrapped around her ankle. Then, the woman felt a strong tug backward, followed by an electric shock.

The masked woman fell back. She felt two other things wrapped both her wrists. And finally, something else wrapped her other ankle. Each time whatever wrap her, she got electrocuted. The woman screamed each time. She was stretched in four directions.

She looked and saw that four Nihils used shock whips on her. She struggled but couldn't move. The Nihils laughed at her plight.

"Rawhhhhh," said the leader as he was about to land. The axe was ready to sink its blade into the flesh of its prey. But, it sunk into oak instead.

"Yeawwwh!" Sam screamed as he shielded the woman with the door. High on adrenaline, Sam had found it easy to pick up the door that had broken off its hinges. The door splintered over the woman, but she was safe. Sam flew back from the force.

When he realized who stopped him, the leader refocused his rage on Sam.

"I'll kill you!"

He raised his axe again as he was over Sam.

"Nooooo!"

The woman pulled her right arm towards herself. One Nihil fell face down. The shock whip's grip loosened. She pulled her left leg towards herself. Another Nihil fell back. The other shock whip unwrapped her leg too. Before the two remaining Nihils could shock her again, the woman swung her body and they bonked their heads.

She quickly pulled out a small metal bar from the side of her pants. The bar flashed and became a gleaming sword. She dashed toward the leader.

Her sword clanged against the axe's beard. The axe flew up. She seamlessly sliced off his robotic arm. The leader looked at her in shock. His stature shrunk. His rage melted into fear. His eyes darted around, and his lips quivered. He bowed before the masked woman.

"Please, don't hurt me!"

When he pleaded, his hand clasped one of her feet. He was shaking.

"Go!"

With that command, he quickly got up.

"Run," he ordered.

All the Nihils fled, leaving their weapons behind as well as the robotic arm.

She went over to Sam.

"Are you all right?"

"Yes," Sam replied. "Thank you. You came at the right time. How can I ever re—."

She disappeared. Sam just stood there wondering. He looked up.

"Thank you, Lord. Thank you!"

14

THE THREAT AMONG US

"Did you see this?!"

A man showed the video of the fight between the masked woman and the Nihils before the local municipal Gaia Council. The man was tall, somewhat muscular. He was remarkably handsome, somewhere in his late thirties to mid-forties, Caucasian but had a Mediterranean tinge. He wore a high-end business suit. And on his left lapel, he had an emblem of the scarlet seven-headed dragon, which was the symbol for Dragon Corp.

One of the councilmembers responded.

"From what I see, Nihils were trying to attack this woman, but she's dodging them. Skillfully, I must say."

The man from Dragon Corp shook his head.

"How about this?"

He played more of the video. He showed them footage of when the woman threw the knife into robotic hand. Then, he showed where she sliced off the robotic arm.

"Oh my...", said another councilmember.

"Still don't believe me. Let me read from their Scriptures. I'll show you how dangerous these people are."

The man pulled out a Bible from his briefcase. Many in the council have never seen a Bible before. He flipped through some pages till he found the passage he was looking for.

" 'If a man lies with a male, as with a woman, both of them have committed an abomination. They shall surely be put to death. Their blood shall be upon themselves.' "

He looked up at the council but kept the Bible open.

"There you go. What? Two consenting two adult men, who love each other and want to show their intimacy toward each other. They call them an abomination and call for the death penalty for it. How backwards and barbaric is this?!"

Some in the council looked at each other in horror and shook their heads.

"Oh, I'm not finished yet. Here's a good one.

He turned to another passage and read it.

" 'If a man finds a lady who is a virgin, who is not pledged to be married, grabs her, and lies with her, and they are found; then the man who lay with her shall give to the lady's father fifty shekels of silver. She shall be his wife, because he has humbled her. He may not put her away all his days. A man shall not take his father's wife, and shall not uncover his father's skirt.' "

When the man finished reading, he threw the Bible onto the table where his briefcase was. He looked up at the council again. He shook his head. His hands were open wide. The man had a disgusted look on his face.

"What the hell is that! A woman who's been raped but has to stay married to the rapist. That's torture! What a sadistic, misogynistic, homophobic god do these people worship. When are we going to wake up?!"

The council murmured among each other. They shook their heads and exchanged troubled looks. But, a council woman looked at the man.

"Um...Mr..."

"Aesar, Eron C. Aesar."

"Mr. Aesar, your accusations are off-base. You're citing from the Old Testament and Christians follow the New Testament."

Eron had indignant look on his face.

"What are you, one of them?"

"No, I'm not. I'm Jewish. Christians may pick and choose from what to follow in the Old Testament. But, they follow the New Testament and Jesus of Nazareth. I've worked with this church on improving the lives of this community. Based on my dealings with them—and I don't agree with their beliefs—none of your accusations hold water."

"Oh....", responded Eron smugly. "So, you hold these views then I just cited?"

"Nnn-ooo," the woman said as she shook her head. "But that's another discussion on how I view the Scriptures. The point is you're way off base."

"Oh...am I?"

He went to the table. Eron picked up the Bible. He opened up to find the passage he was looking for.

"So, you're saying they follow Jesus. Let's see what this Jesus says."

"If anyone comes to me, and doesn't disregard his own father, mother, wife, children, brothers, and sisters, yes, and his own life also, he can't be my disciple. Whoever doesn't bear his own cross, and come after me, can't be my disciple."

"Wow! Is that the loving Jesus they want us to believe?"

The council remained silent.

"Let's get a load of what He says here. This concerns me."

Eron flipped through the Bible again till he got to the spot to prove his point. He read it slowly.

"I came to throw fire on the earth. I wish it were already kindled. ... Do you think that I have come to give peace in the earth? I tell you, no, but rather division."

Eron closed the Bible but still held it in his hand.

"What kind of talk is this," he asked as he was waving the Bible in his hand.

"Throw the earth into the fire?! Our precious Gaia that we're trying to save from ourselves destroyed? Our Mother who sustains us, burned up?!"

Eron went into a maniac frenzy as he spoke.

"And 'this Jesus' doesn't want peace but division! Their own founder doesn't want peace and life, but division and destruction! I'm not making this up. It comes from their very own Scriptures!"

Eron frantically and repeatedly pointed his index finger onto the Bible.

"My Gaia! What kind of people are these?! They have been responsible for the Crusades, which killed millions of people. They have tormented, tortured, burned, and kill many throughout history who don't fit their orthodoxy. And they've denied women choosing what they want with their own bodies. They denied martial rights to our same-sex families and people who wanted to go beyond their narrow view of marriage! Do you want these people around! These are extremists, I tell you! EXTREMISTS!!"

Eron flung the Bible. It bounced off a wall and slid onto the floor.

"Mr. Aesar," said the chair of the council. "You accuse these Christians as extremists, but you are showing yourself to be an extremist. A part of the Religious Moderation Act isn't to speak such inflammatory remarks of a faith or a religious view, unless someone from that group is present to defend or explain their views."

"Ahh," responded Eron with his finger raised. "But, it's also the law," he said as he swung around and pointed his finger at the chair, "to report any radical activity from a faith or religion with evidence. I just gave you evidence! What else do you need?!"

"You seem knowledgeable about their faith," chimed in a councilmember. He was an older white male, white haired. He wore steel rimmed glasses. "How do you know so much?"

"It's because," Eron turned to the councilmember and responded calmly, "I was one of them at one point. My mother was a devout Christian. My father walked out on my brother and I when we were little. My mother taught us the Bible. She took us to Church. I participated in the Sunday school. It was all well and good till one night."

Eron started to cry. Tears fell from his eyes, but he continued to speak.

"I woke up to hot flames engulfing the little house we lived in. I shook my brother to wake him up. We tried to get out of the room, but the door was too hot to open. We went for the window. We jumped out of it. When we were outside, we looked for our mother, but she wasn't there."

Eron stopped. He wailed for a minute. Some in the council cried too, including the old man. Eron wiped away the tears and composed himself. He spoke again.

"When I looked at the burning house, it collapsed. I screamed 'Mom!' as I helplessly reached out for her. My brother buried his head in my shoulders crying. We didn't know what to do, except for one thing: go to the church. So, we knocked on their door, but no one answered. My brother and I slept on the doorstep until someone saw us. The church didn't know what to do with us. We bounced around from one family and to the next until we ended up with the pastor and his wife. This man was not like the man you saw on Sundays. He was a horrible, cruel man. His wife was a banshee and a harpy rolled into one. Their dogs were treated better than we were. We did hard labor and given scraps to eat."

The council shook their heads in shame.

"Their children were rotten too. They pushed us around and excluded us from many things. We endured the hardship of these tyrants till one day."

Eron's face shifted from sadness to anger. He gritted and gnashed his teeth and pursed his lips as he continued.

"I caught that demon, they called a pastor, choking my brother. He was younger than me. He tried to do his best to obey, but it was never good enough. That bastard screamed epitaphs at him for not doing something right as he choked him. My brother looked helpless while his life was getting squeezed out of him. I refused to just stand there and let my brother die. I went to the kitchen and grabbed a knife. The banshee tried to stop me, but I slashed her across the chest. And I ran at full force at that tyrant and I stabbed him in the back into one of his kidneys. He dropped my brother. After a few gasps for air, he got up. We ran out of the house. I went one way. My brother went the other way. I never saw him again."

The chair and the council nodded along and some continued to shed tears as he spoke.

"I went to the church to the elders and deacons and tried to explain who these people really are and what I had to do to save my brother. They didn't believe me. They hurled insults at me. They tried to get me arrested. I fled and lived on the streets. I tried to go some other churches, but they didn't help me.

His anger subsided and went back to a calm demeanor.

"So, I abandoned Christianity. And pulled up my bootstraps. I built Dragon Corp to be what it is. I did that. I didn't need Jesus or his lackeys. So, you see, my friends, they are hypocrites at best and dangerous at worst."

The elder councilmember nodded along.

"So what do you propose we should do?" he asked.

Eron grinned. He pushed his neuroputer. An image of a miniature city emitted from his eyes and it appeared in the middle of the council hall.

"We demolish this church along with the rest of the decaying area. It's in a crime ridden area. We then rebuild the area by putting in a Dragon Corp biotech facility. Dragon Corp will partner with The Weshounder Group, the global shopping and retail developer, to build up an exquisite and very expansive shopping city by the facility. Dragon Corp will also partner with Kingman & Queensland International, the global housing and architecture corporation, to build a new community for the workers to live nearby. Jobs! Revenue! Public Safety! Peace of mind! It's a win-win for everyone!"

His tone and demeanor changed to that of a slick salesman.

The chair was a little skeptical of this. He pursed his lips as he heard the presentation. He rubbed his hand on his chin. He fired a volley of his doubt at Eron.

"Isn't this a little self-serving to show us these 'radicals', yet your solution is to take this property and the property nearby and make it your own? And what's going to happen to everyone who lives in this area? What will happen to the few local shops and businesses in this area? Are they going to be able to stay? Is this going to be affordable for the people of this area?"

Eron stopped emitting the proposed corporate paradise from his mind. He grinned again. He donned a smug look. He laughed at the chair.

"You stupid hypocrite! When did you care about these people? Wasn't it you who withheld funding to revitalize this hellhole you call a part of town?"

He pointed his finger at the chair. Eron's eyes pierced through his chicanery. The chair started to tremble in fear.

"So, where did that money go, ladies and gentlemen?" Eron turned around at the council with both his arms wide open. "Do you want to know?"

He quickly spun back towards the chair with his finger pointing and shaking.

"It went in his back pocket! Yes, he took all the money!"

The council was surprised. You could hear murmurs amongst them.

"While this side of town wallows in poverty and sunk further into decay, our trusted chair lives the high life. He used discretionary funds to do in-discretionary things!"

The elder councilmember shook his head.

"Is this true Mr. Chair?"

The chair stood silent, frozen in fear. His darkness was exposed to the light.

"Is it?!"

Still no response.

Eron interrupted the inquisition.

"Ahh, it's not just the chair who needs to be exposed. Many of you are corrupt. I know. I've seen it all. You wouldn't like it if I brought this to the public. But to show I'm not bluffing, let's air out more dirty laundry, shall we?"

Eron pointed his dart of truth at one councilmember. He was a portly fellow but well dressed. The councilman's eyes grew wide. His jaw was open and shaking. What was Eron going to say?

"You, fine sir, are not so fine! You entertain yourself with young ones. From obscene pictures to evil activities, this seemingly upstanding councilmember is a perverted reprobate!"

At that moment, the councilmember hyperventilated from Eron's uncovering of his shameful activities. He clinched his chest. He fell over and died.

Eron looked around the room to see whose skeleton in the closet he would like to drag out. The council cowered at him. Eron's eyes landed on a council woman. She trembled.

The council member was mousey in her demeanor. Her mouth accentuated this appearance.

"You, my dear, there's an old adage: watch out for the quiet ones."

Eron chuckled.

"That's what makes you a great silent killer. Your appearance stealthily covers the deranged murderer you really are!"

Members of the council looked at each other in horror and disbelief. But some kept their head down. They did what they could stay out of the light of Eron.

"Yeah," continued Eron. "Ms. Mousey who doesn't say anything in these meetings is Ms. Manic. Do you want to know what she did?"

No inquiry from anyone.

"Okay, good. Let me tell you. She murdered several people who tried to run against her, because of her lack of representing the people she claims she does. And when some in the media try to expose her questionable ethics and corrupt, they were offed too. You have to wonder why she runs and is elected from her area unopposed."

Eron raised his finger.

"But ahh, that's not the ghastly part. When her husband found out about her dark side, she killed him and hacked him in two."

Eron leaned forward towards her direction. His eyes engaged hers. She remained stone faced.

"How did it feel when your own—"

Eron's voice cracked. Tears flowed down his cheeks and onto the lapel of his suit.

"Your own husband! What kind of jackal of hell are you?!"

The council woman's eyes widened. Her face turned lobster red. The woman's mousey manner dissipated. She became a screaming demon. She quickly pulled out a small metal bar underneath her suit jacket. A sword materialized in her hand. She leapt towards Eron.

Eron quickly hopped back some distance away. He pulled out a gun from his suit jacket. He shot her in the head. The violent leap became an uneventful flop.

"You killed her!" yelled the chair.

"Like you haven't killed someone yourself?! And you didn't kill them in self-defense."

Eron looked at him with askance.

"So, don't give me this phony indignation, you hypocrite!"

"Why are you doing this to us," the chair asked Eron sheepishly.

"Doing what?! Exposing you for what you are: a bunch of ravenous snakes. There's a threat among us, yet you are too corrupt to see it!"

The first council woman, who questioned Eron earlier, shook her head and looked at him with renewed skepticism.

"This all may be so with this council," she interrupted with her hand extended behind at the council. "But what gives you the right to monitor us? You shouldn't have access to surveillance files! You need to –"

"Oh, my dear but I do," Eron rebuked her with a grin. "You see. Unlike you all, who are power drunken fiends who like to obfuscate the law to the general public, so you can practice your corruption unchecked, I know my rights as a citizen. Though the government can conduct surveillance if they feel it's necessary, the people can conduct surveillance on the government in kind. This mutual spying was one of the reasons why people formed the United Gaia Council. The former world government before the global war was out of control with power and had no recourse for the people, which is why it crumbled. And the machines you use for your spying are the property of Dragon Corp. You are just leasing them from us. So, we can review the records if we feel we need to. Our only obligation to the government is to tell you ahead of time."

Eron blinked and the council saw the letter Dragon Corp issued to the UGC from their neuroputers. Eron's grin disappeared and look of disapproval replaced when he looked at the council woman.

"Now, my dear, what right you have draining society's precious resources!"

Her skeptical demeanor gave way to that of fear.

"Yes, her son is an undesirable. He's autistic, which is supposed to be aborted, according to the—"

"You leave my son out of this, you soulless bastard!"

Eron talked over her.

"Healthy Populations Act. When she was told her son would be born autistic through screening, instead of doing what's proper for us for sustainability and survival by terminating the pregnancy, she paid off the doctor, so she could keep her son. And then she commits fraud to get her undesirable son all the benefits of our society. How selfish, unfair, and corrupt is that?!"

The woman stood up and pointed her finger at Eron.

"You frickin' jackass! My son is a human being like the rest of us! You hear me!"

Eron grinned again.

"Ahh....so what do we do about this?"

Eron paced around the floor slowly.

"What shall I do with your secrets. Should I report all of you to the media and the Federal Council? Or, will you help me combat this danger, and I will expunge what I have on all of you. The choice is yours."

After a moment, the chair stood up.

"The council moves to vote to demolish this church and the area to allow Dragon Corp, The Weshounder Group, and Kingman & Queensland International to buy the land and proceed with their project," he said meekly.

"All in favor, say 'Aye.' "

"Aye."

"Any nays? Any abstentions?"

None dared to oppose. He hammered his gavel.

"Okay, the notices shall be issued to the area with a set date for all to vacate."

Eron nodded in approval.

"Thank you for your service to Gaia."

He walked out of the meeting hall.

A janitor stood nearby and shook his head.

"This isn't good."

15

LOOKING CLOSER

As Eron was walking down the hall to leave the building, the janitor subtly followed him. He hadn't cleaned this part of the hall yet, so it didn't look suspicious to the cameras as he swept and mopped the floor behind Eron.

Eron was almost at the entrance. When the janitor saw the camera bots and guard bots outside, he stopped following.. But the janitor discreetly kept his eye on him. As Eron left the building, something strange happened. When he passed by the machines, they all flickered and shut down. The janitor came closer to the entrance but dared not to leave. Eron turned the corner. The janitor moved toward the row of windows to see where he was going.

Eron stopped when he saw a group of Nihils come towards him. They were the same ones who attacked Sam and the mystery woman. The leader was still missing his robotic arm. The Nihils didn't seem to faze Eron. He and the leader of the Nihils began to talk to each other.

The janitor discreetly moved closer to the entrance. He unscrewed the top of his mop and a small drone, which was the size of a penny, floated out of it. The janitor nodded his head and the drone flew towards Eron and the Nihils. It hovered a distance from them.

The janitor gently tapped one of his eyes with his hand, and several cameras emerged on the surface of the drone. He then tapped his ear and several microphones came out too. The janitor pushed his temple on the side of the same eye to zoom in the cameras. He also pushed the tragus of the ear to amplify the microphones.

"Here you go," said Eron. He transferred credits to the leader of the Nihils.

"Thank you," said the leader. "We needed the money."

"No problem, I'm a man of my word," said Eron. "Besides, this isn't about money or fighting. This is about dealing with a threat to society. And finally, I got the council to get off their rear ends to do something about them."

"Yes, indeed," said the burly fellow. "We need to deal with these Christians. They're not a good bunch. And the council don't fare much better than them. But it's nice to get to buy a new robotic arm. How did you get to those jokers on the council to do something?"

"Don't ask."

The Nihil leader nodded.

"Boss, what about us?" asked one of the Nihils.

The leader turned around and gave them an annoyed look.

"Here! You're like a bunch of mangy dogs looking for food."

He disbursed the credits amongst the group but kept most of it for himself.

"Sorry, they don't get the bigger picture, Mr. Aesar."

"It's okay," replied Eron as he placed his hand on the Nihil's shoulder. It was the one with the missing arm. "Many people who are under us don't see it. That's why we lead, and they follow."

The leader nodded in agreement.

"You didn't have to try hard to get damaging video of these Christians. It fell into our lap. All you had to do was cause trouble. It was all good timing. I was waiting for a time to bust them. And now, we did it. We just had to set them up. It pays to tie the United Gaia Council up with the fact that Dragon Corp owns the surveillance equipment and that I have caught these corrupt politicians red-handed.

The janitor raised his eyebrows when he heard Eron's confession.

"Yes, finally we use their corruption to get this council to do what's right for society," the leader said. "Though we disagree on many things, we were able to put our differences aside to deal with a common enemy."

"Yes," replied Eron as he placed his hand again on the Nihil's armless shoulder. "That's the spirit of humanity. We don't need their backward ways and their barbaric good. We need to move forward. By the way, don't worry about paying for the arm. It's on Dragon Corp. Come in and I'll give you an upgrade. And if you want, you can join me as head of security. What do you say?"

"I think, Mr. Aesar, this is a start of a beautiful friendship," said the burly man as he shook Eron's hand.

"Boss, this is a mega-corporation," protested the Nihil. "They are the enemy. We can't join them."

"Shut up! You know nothing. You can't see the bigger picture. And who says you will join Dragon Corp. I'm doing bigger things now than being just a street thug."

"Look!"

One of the Nihils spotted the drone. His robotic eye implant zoomed in to confirm what he saw.

"Someone is spying on us!" yelled the leader.

The janitor was scared. He moved his head to the side and retrieved the drone.

Eron tapped his temple. Something that looked like goggles appeared over his eyes. It helped him zoomed on the fleeing drone. He pulled out his gun and shot it. The drone exploded with a quick metallic hissing sound.

"Look around to see who it is," ordered Eron.

The Nihils rushed around but couldn't find anyone.

"We couldn't find no one, Mr. Aesar," said one of the Nihils.

"Then, we must make act quickly," said Eron. "For our enemy is onto us. Nigil, have your gang execute plan B. I will upgrade you as soon as possible. We will make sure no one hinders our progress. We must make our stand for Gaia and her children."

Nigil, the leader of the Nihils, nodded in acquiescence to Eron's command.

"It will be done."

The janitor quickly hid into a nearby supply closet by the entrance.

16

ECHOES FROM THE PAST

"Mr. Mayor, please open the door," pleaded the janitor. He rapped on the door of the mayor's house.

The mayor wasn't there at the meeting. He has been sick for months and has been only seen a handful of times. The council chair has been running things since.

No one came to the door. The janitor knocked frantically on the door. "Please, it's urgent!"

Still no answer. The janitor tried to look inside from the window at the top of the door but couldn't see anything. He knocked again. No one came.

The janitor shook his head and turned away. When he started to head for the sidewalk, he heard the metallic hiss of a door opening. He quickly turned around. There was no one there.

The janitor went up to the door. He peered inside the house. He didn't see anybody there. The janitor cautiously stuck his head inside the house. After some time of hesitation, he went inside.

The janitor tipped-toed around the front rooms. He saw no one. He went into the kitchen; he still didn't see anyone. The janitor heard music playing in a room somewhere. It sounded like music from the 20th century. The mayor was an aficionado of music from that era.

Intrigued by the sound of the music, the janitor followed it. The music got louder as he moved towards it. The music sounded like an old-timey jazz with a ragtime sound.

If he found the mayor, he would tell the janitor that this song is called "The Charleston." The mayor would have proceeded in showing him the dance that went with this once famous song. The janitor ended up in a room with stacked of vinyl records and CDs. On top of some tables were a couple of record players and CD players. The source of the song was a reconstructed jukebox on the other side of the room. "The Charleston," with its catchy rhythm, put the janitor at ease. He smiled and felt like dancing. It played another few seconds and then faded away. There was silence. The janitor's era of good feelings evaporated into the ether.

Another song broke the silence. It was from the 1960's and had a very haunting intro. If the mayor were here, he would tell the janitor the song is called "For what it's worth" by Buffalo Springfield.

The haunting intro and piercing lyrics followed.

He felt uneasy. It felt like this song was like a warning message for him. Click.

The janitor's blood went ice cold and he felt a pit in his stomach. He knew that sound. He turned around. It was a man dressed in black armor. His face was covered in a black ski mask. He held a gun and pointed at the janitor.

The masked man squeezed the trigger. The janitor closed his eyes. But when the man fired, Sam tackled him, and the gun shot upward.

Sam knocked the gun out of the man's hand, but the man overpowered Sam. The janitor was puzzled and scared at what was going on. He took a couple of steps back. Suddenly, he felt someone clasp a metal bar against his throat. He felt a violent squeeze.

He was trying to gasp for air but couldn't. The janitor saw the man further thwarted Sam's valiant attempt when the man reclaimed his gun and pistol whipped him. He pointed the gun at Sam. The janitor started to lose consciousness from the lack of air. He stopped fighting and surrendered to despair. The janitor thought it'll all be over soon. His eyes drooped. But then, something reinvigorated him.

The same mystery woman who saved Sam before knocked the masked man in the back of the head with a wooden staff. The janitor violently moved his head back. The grip loosened and the bar fell. The janitor took a deep breath and spun around with a punch. It landed on the jaw of the masked man behind him. The man fell back. Blood seeped through the mask from his nose and mouth.

The masked woman picked Sam up. But then four more masked men came. Three were armed. One of them had metal hands. He was bigger and more muscular than the rest. As for the other three, one had a metal whip, one had a sword, and the other had an extendable metal bat.

The metal fisted one charged at the woman and Sam with his fist out. She pushed Sam out of the way and quickly ducked. The man punch landed into the wall.

The one with the metal whip aimed for the janitor. Razor talons popped out on the sides of the whip. He dodged the menacing lash but got hit on his shoulder. One of the talons ripped into his shirt and into his flesh.

"Ahhh!" screamed the janitor. He fell. The metal whip man was about the strike again. But Sam picked up the pistol and whipped him in the back of the head. He fell down next to the gunman.

"Thanks," said the janitor. "Ahh!"

The janitor held the top of his arm and shoulders. Blood seeped through his fingers as he held his wound. It was deep. Sam started to take off his shirt to wrap around the janitor's wound.

"Look out!"

The masked man with the sword came charging at them. The masked woman's foot swept out in front of the man. As he fell, the sword flew out of his hand. The man with the bat caught it.

"Ha, ha, ha."

"We got to get out of here," Sam said.

The woman helped Sam pick up the janitor.

"Are you okay," she asked Sam.

"Yeah, just a little pain."

His nose was bleeding from the pistol whip.

"Watch out!"

The man with the metal fists pulled his hand out of the wall. He made another charge—fist forward. The woman and Sam, while holding the janitor, quickly dodged the charge. The man's fist landed on another masked man's skull, cracking it.

"This is like an old, bad video game," the janitor said, only half-joking.

"There's too many of them!" Sam exclaimed.

The woman let go of the janitor.

"Guys, close your eyes!"

She threw a flash bomb. It exploded in mid-air.

"Arrggghh, I can't see!" the masked men screamed.

"We can't get through them," said Sam.

Another song played in the background. Surprisingly, during the melee no one smashed the jukebox or the speakers. It was "White Room" by Cream.

Then, it dawned on the janitor.

"I don't think these songs are random, I believe the mayor is or was trying to tell us something. Look!"

He pointed with his uninjured arm at the black curtains ahead of them draping the entrance to what appeared to be a white room. Above the curtains was a picture of an old train stopped in front of a station, with people getting off and on.

Sam and the masked woman didn't question the janitor's theory. They went towards the curtains. When they got close, what appeared to be a room was just a wall.

"What?!" exclaimed Sam.

"Just keep moving forward. Trust in the Lord," replied the woman.

Then, the curtains and the walls opened. Ahead of them was a narrow path. There was light on the path to show Sam, the masked woman, and the janitor where to go.

"After them!" cried out the masked man with the metal hands. The blinding effects from the flash bomb had faded.

"They're gaining on us!" cried Sam. "We're not going to make it!"

"Sam," replied the masked woman. "Trust in the LORD with all your heart, and do not lean on your own understanding. In all your ways acknowledge him, and he will make your paths straight."

Sam's anxiety ebbed a bit when he heard these words. But, how did she know his name?

"Lord, may you be a light unto our feet and a light unto our path," she prayed.

"Look up ahead," said the janitor.

There was an opening and light up ahead. They kept going until they got to the opening. Their determination wasn't broken by the howls of the men behind them. When they got to the opening, they had to take a leap. They landed on a very soft padding.

The men didn't catch up to them. When they leapt, the walls closed and crushed them.

Sam looked upward and cried, "The LORD is my strength and song, and he is become my salvation."

17

NO TIME FOR QUESTIONS

Sam again offered his shirt to tie up the janitor's deep wound. From a gash that deep, it was a miracle that janitor didn't lose more blood than he did. All three got off the landing.

"Thank you. How did you know to come?" asked the janitor.

"I didn't," replied Sam. "I felt the Holy Spirit lead to me to go inside the house."

The janitor didn't know what that meant. He could tell that Sam was religious.

Sam continued, "When I saw you were danger, I just helped."

"Well, regardless how you got there, thank you."

"We need to get you to the doctor."

"No, it will be okay," protested the janitor. "Ahh."

"You need to get that taken care of."

"We need to find the mayor. Do you know where he is?"

"No, sorry I don't," said Sam as he shrugged his shoulders and shook his head lightly.

"We need to find him soon."

"Why? By the way, you were very insightful in guessing what the songs were trying to tell us."

"That's what I'm afraid of. It might be the mayor's soul data."

Soul data, as it was called, were machines that recorded algorithms of your personality and would try to mimic the decisions and say things you would do if it weren't around. Not always, but soul data was typically used by people who were dying, so they could live on virtually. Soul data had its flaws though. It could corrupt over time and someone could hack into the machines that had your data and either tamper with it or destroy it. But people would use it if they felt they had unfinished business to do after they were in the grave.

"What's going on?"

"The church in this area and the community is in danger. Dragon Corp along with two other major mega-corporations will take over and rebuild this area in their image."

Sam still wasn't sure what was going on and why this janitor needed to find the mayor.

"Where will the people go," continued the janitor. "How will people afford it? They will have to be exploited by these vultures if they want to stay around. Wait a minute, you're—you're the guy who was attacked by those Nihils in the front of the church!"

Sam nodded.

"Yes, yes, I am the one. But I still don't know what's going on."

"They set up the attack to show how radical this church was and to show how dangerous the area is."

"Who's they? Who's setting things up? Were they the same ones who attacked us in the mayor's house?"

"There's no time for questions, Sam. That's your name, right?"

Sam nodded.

"Speaking of knowing my name, how did you know mine?"

Sam was asking the woman this question. He turned towards her, but she was gone.

"Where did she go?"

"I don't know, but we gotta go."

"Where?"

18

GRAVE MESSAGE

"Come! Let's go. I know where to find the mayor."

A message appeared on the janitor's neuroputer. It was a message from the mayor telling the neighborhood to come to the amphitheater behind the community center. Sam followed the janitor. He seen others come out of their homes and shops going in the same direction too.

When they got to the amphitheater, Sam saw Beverly, George, and Nadine. He waved at them. They motioned him to come over. The janitor disappeared among the crowd. Sam never saw him again. Sam had so many questions in his head.

"Do you know what's going on," Sam asked his friends.

"We're hoping to find out," Nadine replied.

Beverly sat next to Sam. They were facing a podium in the center of the theater. There was a metallic orb resting on the podium. The orb had a bluish crystalline circle on top. A bluish-white light emerged from the circle. An image of a man, the same color, appeared. When people saw it, some started to mourn. To them, the mayor was the only bulwark against the tide of tyranny and corruption.

Though the mayor didn't have much power, he would do what he could to do stop the UGC's intrusive nature. He would not enforce unjust and tyrannical laws. He wasn't corrupt. He was honest. The mayor was a like a rare gem amongst this government. People were getting anxious because he decided not to seek reelection after four terms of office. He told his constituents that if he ran forever, he would be no better than the power he opposed. However, in his last term, he has been absent a lot because he's been ill. Some have suspected that the government was trying to kill him.

"It's the mayor's soul data," some said. "He must be dead."

Then the soul image of the mayor began to speak.

"People of this community," he said. His voice sounded somewhat metallic and hollow. Some continued to mourn.

"If you are seeing this, then I'm either dead or unable to speak in person. Please do not mourn for me but pay attention to the message at hand."

Sam and Beverly looked at each other briefly wondering what the mayor's soul data was going to say.

"It has come to my attention that this community is in danger."

People looked at each other, whispered to each other what was going on.

"Dragon Corp, along with the Weshounder Group and the Kingman & Queensland International will demolish this area and rebuild it into their image."

Sam turned to Beverly.

"Do you know about this?"

"No."

They both turned back towards the mayor's soul data.

"Eron C. Aesar has strong-armed the local UGC council to comply. Unfortunately, he used convoluted laws to accomplish this for the three mega-corporations. He has used this video."

The soul data showed the video of the confrontation between the Nihils and Sam and the masked woman.

"And he has tried to twist the Bible to make the church look dangerous."

Another video showed up Eron's indictment against Christianity to the council.

"Wait a minute!" someone yelled. "You mean tell us that it was the church's fault for this?!"

The soul data didn't respond to the question. Then, the soul data faded somewhat. An image of a masked man flickered. It was the same one Sam saw before on TV when he was in the hospital.

"Listen, everyone. It's not what it seems...."

The mayor's soul data came back. The Janitor, as this cryptic journalist was called, couldn't interrupt the transmission.

Beverly held Sam's hand. They looked at each other. Both thought about what will happen next.

"Guys, we better get out of here," said George. They saw that some in the community gave them a cold stare, for they knew who George was. Some started coming towards them.

"What should we do," said the soul data. "There are some ways we can respond..."

Sam, Beverly, George, and Nadine gracefully exited out of there. But they knew that trouble was coming like a storm on the horizon.

19

FURY OF THE BEAST

"Many people seek the face of a ruler, but it is from the LORD that one receives justice," said Sam at the pulpit at the church.

Sam and Beverly were taking turns preaching while George and Nadine were on their honeymoon. A couple of days after the soul data spoke at the amphitheater, they got married. Sam, Beverly, and others told the newlywed couple to get away for a while. George and Nadine needed to just spend time with each other and God.

"This has been a fundamental flaw in politics. Rather seeking God's counsel and justice, people seek a human leader instead. They hope the leader can protect them from harm or be an advocate for them against oppressive elites."

Sam looked up at the camera bot crawling around. He had disdain for it, especially after it drove George to the point of suicide. He stared at it briefly and moved his eyes back to the congregation.

"Now leaders and governments are ordained as God's sword of justice—as mentioned in Romans 13. Let me read it. 'Let every soul be in subjection to the higher authorities, for there is no authority except from God, and those who exist are ordained by God. Therefore, he who resists the authority, withstands the ordinance of God; and those who withstand will receive to themselves judgment. For rulers are not a terror to the good work, but to the evil. Do you desire to have no fear of the authority? Do that which is good, and you will have praise from the same, for he is a servant of God to you for good. But if you do that which is evil, be afraid, for he doesn't bear the sword in vain; for he is a servant of God, an avenger for wrath to him who does evil. Therefore, you need to be in subjection, not only because of the wrath, but also for conscience' sake. For this reason, you also pay taxes, for they are servants of God's service, attending continually on this very thing. Therefore, give everyone what you owe: if you owe taxes, pay taxes; if customs, then customs; if respect, then respect; if honor, then honor.' "

The people had heard this passage often quoted by ministers in support of the State.

"Also, in 1 Peter, it says we must obey the ruling authorities. 'Therefore subject yourselves to every ordinance of man for the Lord's sake: whether to the king, as supreme; or to governors, as sent by him for vengeance on evildoers and for praise to those who do well.' "

Sam looked down for a moment and looked back up at the people.

"But," he said through pursed lips, "history shows us that rulers and governments are the oppressors more than the arbiters of justice. However, the Scriptures tell us otherwise. So, where does that leave us as Christians?"

The congregation were shocked at Sam. They knew this and may have mentioned it to each other in conversations or Bible studies but never heard it from the pulpit.

"What does Scripture say? Let's go to some other examples."

He opened to Acts 5, where Peter was put in prison for preaching Christ to the people and an angel freed him.

"You see, Peter and the apostles had run-ins with the religious leaders, because, as you know, they were against Christ. Let's read on. 'When they had brought them, they set them before the council. The high priest questioned them, saying, "Didn't we strictly command you not to teach in this name? Behold, you have filled Jerusalem with your teaching, and intend to bring this man's blood on us." But Peter and the apostles answered, "We must obey God rather than men.' "

The congregation continued to listen to this scandalously true message. This was a message that started to resonate with the people.

"You see, despite the Sanhedrin's commands to not preach the name of Jesus, the apostles' obeyed their Lord's command to go and make disciples—as mentioned in Matthew 28. You might say, 'That's fine and dandy, but these are religious leaders not civil leaders.' Okay, I'll show an example of defying civil government."

He went to the third of the book of Daniel. He read the story of how King Nebuchadnezzar set up a golden image and commanded his subjects to worship it. But Shadrach, Meshach, and Abednego wouldn't do it.

Sam continued, "Let's pay attention to these few verses. 'Then Nebuchadnezzar in rage and fury commanded that Shadrach, Meshach, and

Abednego be brought. Then these men were brought before the king. Nebuchadnezzar answered them, "Is it on purpose, Shadrach, Meshach, and Abednego, that you don't serve my god, nor worship the golden image which I have set up? Now if you are ready whenever you hear the sound of the horn, flute, zither, lyre, harp, pipe, and all kinds of music to fall down and worship the image which I have made, good; but if you don't worship, you shall be cast the same hour into the middle of a burning fiery furnace. Who is that god that will deliver you out of my hands?" Shadrach, Meshach, and Abednego answered the king, "Nebuchadnezzar, we have no need to answer you in this matter. If it happens, our God whom we serve is able to deliver us from the burning fiery furnace; and he will deliver us out of your hand, O king. But if not, let it be known to you, O king, that we will not serve your gods or worship the golden image which you have set up.' "

The camera bot stopped crawling around and focused on Sam. He gave it no regard anymore.

"So, you have men of God disobeying the king because he wanted them to sin by bowing down to idols. You have the apostles disregard the religious leaders' command to not tell others about Jesus. And history shows us that governments are oppressive, unjust, and tyrannical. Yet, you have parts of Scripture that tell us to obey the governing authorities. Do we have a contradiction?!"

The people wondered about this too. They whispered among themselves.

"Perish the thought! It's not God's word that contradicts reality but humans in government who contradict God!"

"Amen," shouted the congregation. They clapped and shouted praises to God.

"This institution that God ordained as His sword of justice on earth, many times people who rule have wielded it as a hatchet of horror, injustice, tyranny, and violence. Do I need to cite examples of in this history?! We'd be here all day. I would encourage you to do your research on this. But these rulers are really doing the work of their master, Satan. Let's read Matthew 4, shall we."

Sam read the story when Jesus was tempted by Satan in the wilderness.

"So, let me note this verse I'm about to read. 'Again, the devil took him to an exceedingly high mountain, and showed him all the kingdoms of the world, and their glory. He said to him, "I will give you all of these things, if you will fall down and worship me." Then Jesus said to him, "Get behind me, Satan! For it is written, 'You shall worship the Lord your God, and you shall serve him only.' "

The camera bot continued to zoom in on Sam. It stayed where it was at. It was trying to check and cross-reference for Sam Lysander in any government databases. But, it was confused the robot because Sam Lysander was officially deceased. It sent out a warning message for law enforcement to come anyway but be on stand-by. The congregation looked on in fear at the intense stare the spider-like machine gave at Sam. But, he didn't care. The camera bot was still trying to reconcile how a dead person would be speaking to them.

Sam asked for the Spirit to guide his actions and words as he spoke on this issue. He knew he was being scrutinized, but he was carefully following down the Narrow Path of his Lord.

"Now we know that Satan is the father of lies, and it's possible that he was lying to Jesus that he owned the world's kingdoms. But in this case, let's go to some passages that might back up that he is lord over governments."

Sam turned to another part in the Scripture to make his case.

"Even if our Good News is veiled, it is veiled in those who are dying; in whom the god of this world has blinded the minds of the unbelieving, that the light of the Good News of the glory of Christ, who is the image of God, should not dawn on them."

Sam looked up from the text.

"Who is the god of this world? It's Satan. For those who are confused by this, when the Scriptures say the world, it's not this planet. God owns it like He owns all the planets in this vast cosmic expanse we call the Universe."

"Amen!"

"We are talking about the society in this world. It's the mechanism that it operates, which includes government. Satan is really behind it. Let's me take you to another passage."

The police were on their way to the church. The robot raised the alert level to urgent, but it was still confused how a supposed dead man could speak. A mechanized armored unit followed in tow. The officers suited up into these mechanized armor suits.

Sam went to Revelation 13 and read the entire passage.

"Now they have been a variety of opinions of who these beasts are throughout our history. I think it's reasonable to believe that the beast of the sea represents the world's kingdoms. If you look at Daniel 7—and let me take you there—you'll notice that the individual beasts make up the picture of this beast in Revelation." Sam took them to Daniel 7 and read the passage.

❧

The police sped towards the church. But as they were racing to stop Sam's dangerous rhetoric, someone shot the side of one of their vehicles. It came somewhere from a window above in an abandoned building.

"We've been hit!" yelled an officer in the passenger seat. The shot pierced a hole into the vehicle's armor. The police stopped. Another shot fired. This time, it hit a mechanized suit. The officer inside it died.

"Someone has armor-piercing bullets!" yelled another officer as they got out.

"What?! I thought they were illegal," replied the officer who noted the first shot.

"WATCH OUT!!!!!"

Another officer nearby split into two from another bullet. Someone fired these bullets at a fierce velocity.

"It's like a mini rail-gun."

"We're sitting ducks!"

Then, someone high up from another building opened fired. The blast caused an armored police carrier to explode.

"It's coming from up there," said an officer in a mechanized suit.

Another shot zoomed toward the suit, hitting it in the back. The mechanized suit fell on its hands and knees.

"I've been hit badly... God help us all ..."

Then, the mechanized suit fell facedown, and the officer died.

"We're getting picked off here!"

The police officers who were inside the vehicles stepped out and used the doors as a shield to protect themselves while they were trying to fire back. But, their protection was in vain when the bullets sliced through the doors and pierced through their flesh.

"Help, we need backup," pleaded an officer on her helmet's comlink. "We're being butchered...argghh..."

Her helmet split and her brain splattered.

"Noooo!" yelled her partner. He quickly picked up the high-powered rifle inside the armored vehicle. He fired on the sniper above. The sniper fell forward out the window and onto the street. The sniper wore a black trench coat with a red Circle A.

"Anarchists!" cried the officer.

Vocal anarchists did not engage in violence. They used peaceful alternatives to the society. They were first to condemn such actions against the government or the mega-corporations. They long contend these are provocateurs who are trying to discredit them. Even the cryptic investigative journalists, the Janitor, lend some credence to this idea. But, the government didn't believe the anarchists and would go after them anyway.

One of the remaining mechanized units managed to blast the other sniper. There were only two mechanized units and ten officers standing after the carnage was over, just one-third of those originally on their way to the church.

Their relief ended when they heard metallic, high pitched howls, followed by growls. The cops looked up and saw several robots that looked like jackals from the rooftops. Their jaws were open, exposing their razors steel teeth. Their red eyes gleamed. The jackals howled and growled again.

The police froze. Their courage dissipated.

"Retreat!" yelled a commanding officer. The police tried to escape but a large group of people dressed as jackals armed with hatchets and machetes rushed onto the police in mass. They howled and growled when they attacked. The robotic jackals dove onto the police in the mech suits. They ripped the suits from limb to limb. And then devoured the officers inside. The human jackals did the same to the rest of the cops.

"So, what does that mean for us? Are we supposed to pick up arms and overthrow the government?! Is Scripture schizophrenic with this issue?"

Sam looked around the congregation and at the robotic spider above.

"No! It's not our call to get entangled with such ideas. We are here to promote the Kingdom of God."

The congregation clapped.

"We are to obey the rulers, because, though they may mean evil at times, God can use them for good and for justice. It's like what Joseph said to his brothers after their father died. Though they meant to do evil when they sold him into slavery, God turned this situation around to save them and their families from famine."

Then, Sam raised his arm and pointed his finger at the camera bot, while speaking to his brothers and sisters.

"And though these rulers are corrupt, and this thing is intrusive, we will put up with it and obey their decrees. Because we are to keep our eyes on the prize, which is to obey our Lord's call, when He was about to ascend to

His throne, He said to make disciples of all nations! Jesus put up with suffering, injustice, torture, and death to tear that wall down between God and people! And we are to have that same attitude when we bring the message of hope and restoration!"

People stood up and cheered and shouted "Amen, Hallelujah, Praise Jesus!"

The camera bot cancelled its urgency for police to put down a possible rebellion. There was no response from the police squadron that was on its way.

❧

The entire battalion lie dead, bashed, bloodied, with some of their half-eaten limbs scattered on the street. The mob of people dressed as jackals decapitated them and stuck their heads onto wooden poles, which they pounded into the street. The armored vehicles were smashed up and whatever weapons and equipment they found was taken. But some of these jackals, who became followers of Christ, didn't participate in the carnage. They gathered at the church instead.

❧

The spider sent the signal again but still no response. So, it sent the cancelled call to the nearby command center. And the command center confirmed the emergency was over. The camera bot didn't move. It seemed to be frozen.

"But," Sam said with his finger pointing upward. "If these rulers tell us to do things that are contrary our King, we must obey Him rather than them. That's when must disobey them and be loyal to God."

The robot spider was confused. It didn't know what to make of Sam said. It seemed contradictory and puzzling. It kept trying to run several algorithms to decipher the message. The robot's central processor kept coming back with a virtual question mark. It tried harder to figure this out, but it kept coming back as a paradox. It kept trying to resolve these words and decide whether to put out a new insurgency call. Not to mention, it was still trying to figure how Sam was alive.

The Christians were still clapping and shouting praises to God. They began singing.

"Look out!" cried Sam.

The robot crashed onto the floor of the sanctuary.

20
WHEN LIGHT GIVES HEAT

Hordes of people stormed the church. They smashed the windows with whatever they could find. Some created a makeshift battering ram to shatter the door. When they got inside, a few tossed Molotov cocktails. The pews were set ablaze.

The mob splintered into several groups. One jumped onto the stage and broke they found. Someone took an axe and sliced the pulpit. Other groups rushed the upper levels and background. Whatever they deemed valuable, they took. Whatever they thought was worthless, they hurled into the fiery column inside the sanctuary.

The raiders dashed outside the church. Some watched it become an inferno. The remaining stained-glass windows shattered from the fire. The insides quickly collapsed after they left.

Someone etched a giant message at the bottom of the steps to burning building. It said "F—k you extremists, troublemakers, and killers. DIE! GO TO HELL!"

George and Nadine came up to the charred remains of the church building. Their period of newlywed bliss went up in smoke when they slowly looked around at the destruction and saw the scrawled out insult on the sidewalk. Nadine clasped her face with her hands and cried. George embraced her to try to comfort his new bride.

They heard footsteps crunching over the pieces of wood on the floor. Nadine looked up. They turned around. It was Sam and Beverly.

"Do you know what happened," demanded George.

Sam shook his head as he threw a ripped up hymnal book on the floor. Beverly looked around. She put her left hand over her mouth and shook her head at the destruction.

"Do you know anything?!"

"What do you want me say, George," retorted Sam. "The building burned down. I don't know but based on what's written out there, it seems we're targeted for something."

"Well, what did you and Bev do?"

Sam looked at him in indignation. Beverly chose not to acknowledge the question. She was angered that George called her Bev. George and Nadine knew that was a no-no.

"I did something you couldn't do, you coward!"

Nadine went over and slapped Sam in the face.

"That's enough!"

He held his cheek and turned so that his other cheek faced her. Beverly pounced on Nadine and jack-slapped her. Nadine's nose bled.

"How dare you! He preached the unadulterated truth. All your stupid husband cares about is this stupid building! Aghh…!"

Nadine pulled her hair. Beverly knocked her off. The look of love they had for each other morphed into a gaze of hate.

"You, crazy witch! I'm going to kill you!"

"Witch," laughed Beverly. "Look who's talking!"

Before Nadine surrendered to King Jesus, she was a Wiccan and Neo-pagan.

"Arrghh!" screamed George. He lunged towards Beverly and grasped her neck.

Sam dashed toward George and landed a right hook on his face. George fell back a few feet. Sam, in his rage, almost hit Beverly.

"You leave her alone!"

George sat up. He spat out a little bit of blood in his hand. In that small puddle in his palm was a tooth. George looked at Sam and snarled. Beverly and Nadine stopped fighting to see what happened. They both feared what was about to happen.

George leapt up and pummeled Sam with a flurry of fists. George was a boxer in his youth and kept up his fighting form. Sam could only block or evade so many hits. He wasn't able to land a counterpunch. He was no match for the George's nimble footwork. Sam became his punching bag till he collapsed. He gasped for a breath here and there from the streams of blood from his nose and mouth. Blood came up as he coughed for air. Sam's muscles felt like they were hammered by a meat tenderizer. He couldn't tell if anything was broken. Excruciating pain enveloped his body.

"That's enough George," pleaded Nadine. George didn't heed her request.

He stepped on Sam's chest.

"Stop!"

Sam just looked at George in agony. George pressed down Sam's ribcage.

"I'm correcting the mistake that God made by finishing you off!"

"No, George," pleaded Nadine again. She ran over to pull him back. He backhanded her. She whelped and fell back. Her nose bled again. He raised his foot in an angle with his heel pointed at Sam.

"I'm going to strike you with my foot, and I'll bruise you with my heel!"

He gave a devilish howl as he was about to hammer into Sam. But that howl morphed into a scream.

George felt something razor sharp and cold run across his back. It came with such speed that it took a few seconds for the pain to set. He felt warmth flow down his back. George fell back.

He saw Beverly standing over him. She held a tactical knife. The blade was covered in blood. Her face was cold and stern, and her hair flowed when a breeze blew into the lifeless remains of the cathedral.

"Stop!"

George growled. He quickly rolled over and lunged at Beverly. He missed her but swiped the knife from her hand.

"Rarrggh!"

George charged Beverly with her knife, but she sidestepped. George pivoted. He gave her a small gash on her arm. She bled but was unfazed by the wound. Beverly was determined to protect Sam at all costs.

"I know you love this freak, you reprobate! Of course, you would. Shall I tell him?!"

Beverly didn't respond. She hammerblowed the back of his hand that had the knife. It dropped. George screamed. He tried to give her a roundhouse punch with the other hand. She dodged the incoming punch. Beverly grabbed his arm and threw him. He flew into broken pews.

She picked up her knife. She walked towards George.

"Noooo!" screamed Nadine. "Don't hurt him!"

Beverly continued to move towards George. He had a look of despair and fear when Beverly continued towards him. Her face was like stone.

Nadine ran towards Beverly. She jumped on Beverly's back. Beverly pushed her off. Nadine fell back. She tried to tackle Beverly again. Beverly spun around and grabbed Nadine by the shoulders. Nadine was puffy eyed and mascara running down her cheeks. She had blood stains down her lips from the nosebleeds that George and Beverly gave her. Her hair was disheveled.

"You need to trust me. I—" started Beverly. But the she saw George staggering to get up. His fear dissipated. His rage renewed.

Beverly pounced on George. She gripped the sides of George's face with one hand and jerked his head to the left. She drove the knife down on his neck with the other hand.

"Noooo!" screamed Nadine.

Beverly lanced the neuroputer behind George's right ear. He winced. George felt like he got out of an extremely dense fog. He was bewildered.

"I think your neuroputer got hacked. That's why I think these things are bad," said Beverly. "If it were a betting woman, it probably has to do with this arson. But I don't know."

She turned to Nadine with the knife still in her hand. Beverly grabbed her. Nadine resisted. George managed to sit up, but he was in too much pain to go after Beverly. He grasped Beverly's ankle in an effort to stop her.

"Let me go," said Beverly.

"Not until you let Nadine go."

Beverly broke free of his grasp. Nadine tried but couldn't break free of Beverly's. She turned Nadine's head and stabbed the neuroputer behind her right ear. Nadine cried out. Beverly let her go.

Beverly put her knife away and went over to Sam. George crawled over to Nadine and embraced her.

Beverly knelt by Sam. Sam struggled with breathing. He might have had some broken ribs. She gently lifted his head onto her lap. Beverly's finger ran through Sam's hair a couple of times. He held her hand. Beverly sobbed.

"I'm sorry," she cried.

Sam said nothing. He just put his finger on her lips to signal a hush. Beverly lifted his hand from her lips and held it. She then picked him up. Beverly carried him out, leaving the charred building.

"Wait, Beverly, George is hurt. Are you going leave us here?! And don't you want to find out who did this and why?"

Beverly put Sam down momentarily. She pulled out a small pod and kicked it across the floor towards George and Nadine. The pod contained a plasma kit and bandages, which were enough for George's wounds and to replenish any blood he lost. She turned away from them and carried Sam out.

21

DEEP IN EDEN

Sam woke up to find himself in a bed. Gusts of wind and rain rattled the window nearby. From what he could tell, it was sometime in the afternoon.

Sam examined his surroundings. It looked like a log cabin. He saw ahead of him to the right a wooden table pushed against the wall. And pushed against the table were two wooden chairs. Light only came from the window.

It reminded him of the day when he met the King of the Universe. The King ... Sam sighed. All his studying of God's Word, teaching, and doing other "Christian" stuff, Sam forgotten why he did those things—Jesus. He remembered that encounter. It seemed so distant and detached, almost like it never happened. And now, his faith in Christ seemed cold and stale.

"Lord, I'm sorry if I'd forgotten you. I never meant to. All of this is about you. May I remember who you are and why I'm here: it's to do your will, not mine O King."

Sam pulled himself to an upright position in the bed. His chest, especially his ribcage, hurt. Sam remembered the bout he had with George, which almost killed him. Sam shuddered when he recalled the crazed and demon-like fury and strength George possessed. But, Sam wasn't innocent either. His words cut into George deeper than any knife could. Would he ever see him and Nadine again?

Sam confessed before the Lord of his behavior and prayed for George and Nadine. Sam wanted to go to them to reconcile. But Sam wondered if they wanted to see him and Beverly again. Speaking of Beverly, where was she?

The window rattled from the wind. Thunder roared outside. Sam felt scared. He felt so lost. Sam looked upward.

"Lord, open the eyes of my heart again so I can see You. Spirit, guide me once again to Your truth. Father, may I honor You in all things."

Sam felt a hand on his shoulders. The touch felt calm, warm, and familiar. The person knelt beside Sam. Sam turned.

"Lord!"

Jesus knelt on one knee by Sam's bedside. He wasn't in His majestic robes like before. He was in a white robe with a crimson sash wrapped around it.

"Peace be with you, Sam."

Sam looked down.

"O King, I have failed you. My behavior was ...."

Christ gently put his hand up to silence Sam. Sam acquiesced.

"Sam, I know your frame and you are but dust. I understand. I was like you at one point. When I put my deity aside to do what Our Father wanted me to do, I was exposed to all emotions and hardships of humanity."

Sam looked up and objected.

"But Jesus, you never sinned. You couldn't."

King Jesus put His hand on Sam's shoulder. He looked Him in the eye. Jesus's eyes pierced the innermost part of Sam's soul. Great fear but deep comfort enveloped Sam.

"How do you know this? Don't go beyond what you've read, son. How do you know when our enemy tried to discredit me that I couldn't fall down? I was tempted in every way. It was through the Spirit and power of our Father that I overcame sin and death."

Sam trembled. He knew that God could vaporize him. But Sam saw how merciful and restrained God was after Sam interrupted Him. Jesus wasn't angry.

"It doesn't depend on your strength, Sam, to do the will of the Father. You must depend on me. You must ask the Spirit. He will guide you in all truth and He will help you not walk in your flesh. Watch and pray, my son, for the spirit is willing but the flesh is weak. Trust me ... I know."

The Lord patted Sam on the shoulder.

"Keep your eyes on me. I'm not only your King, I'm also your friend. You must remain in me, and I'll remain in you."

Jesus leaned and gave Sam a hug. Sam, overwhelmed with such love, began to cry.

"Though you know how I gave my life to tear down the wall of sin between the world and me, you have no idea how much I love you right now. Trust in me. You know what you need to do. Follow me."

At that moment, Jesus vanished.

22
NEXT STEP

Sam sat up. Tears continued to roll down his cheeks. But he wasn't feeling like a failure anymore. He felt empowered. Sam even forgot about his pain. What would he do next? Jesus told him what to do and that's all he needed.

The storm continued to rage. The howl of the wind got more vicious and the sound of the rain got louder. Thunder roared above. The cabin got darker.

Sam wiped away the tears when he heard someone coming from the hall behind him. A woman appeared beside him. She had a round face and looked like she was of Native American descent. These once strong, rugged people just about vanished, like other indigenous populations. Her salt and pepper hair was pulled back and braided. She looked like she was either in her fifties or sixties. The woman held a wooden tray, which had a cup of tea and a bowl of tomato soup.

"That's quite a storm," she said. "It's unfortunate that we screwed up our climate."

The climate globally was extreme at times. It would get very hot and unbearable or very cold and stormy. Other than trying to end war, the United Gaia Council was created as a world state to combat climate change. But their restrictions, regulations, and taxes only hurt the poor people. The elites would find loopholes or gladly pay the polluting permits and taxes to continue their behavior. What would the incentive be to eliminate the taxes or regulations since the government relied on them to fund themselves?

The mega-corporations, like Dragon Corp, would use geoengineering robots to keep the climate in check and they would receive subsidies doing this.

"Here you go."

"Thank you," said Sam.

Sam sipped the tea and took a spoonful of tomato soup. Both tasted good. His eyebrows raised in delight.

"I'm Elmira," the woman said.

"Sam," replied Sam as he shook her hand.

"I know, Beverly speaks about you, I'm her mother."

She smiled. Sam blushed. Elmira kept grinning.

"Don't worry, she speaks well of you."

It's an honor to meet you, ma'am."

"Wow, what a gentleman, I'm glad I finally had the chance to meet you too."

Sam drank some more tea and sipped his soup. He winced when he moved a bit.

"Are you okay, my son?" asked Elmira.

"Yeah, it's hurts when I move at times."

"I've heard what happened, I'm really sorry."

Elmira turned towards the window. She was concerned about the storm outside.

"This is one of the reasons I stay away from religious institutions. I never liked that fellow anyway. Sorry," she turned to Sam, "that's just my two cents."

"It's okay. If it weren't for Beverly, I would have been dead."

Sam winced some more when he tried to make himself more comfortable.

"Speaking of Beverly, where is she?"

Elmira looked towards the window again. She put her hand on her lips.

"I don't know," she said as she shook her hand. "I'm a little worried."

Elmira walked over to the wooden table ahead. She picked up an envelope. Elmira came back towards Sam.

"This is for you, Sam. It's from Beverly."

She handed the envelope to him. He looked at it. It had his name written in the middle.

"I'll leave you to it," said Elmira. "I'll be back in a bit to see if you need anything."

Elmira went to the window. She looked out for a minute, shook her head, and walked away.

When she left, Sam opened the envelope and pulled out a note. He began to read it.

∾

My dearest friend, Sam,

I pray you recover quick. I left you at my mother's cabin for you for heal and rest till you're ready to leave. I felt I've gotten distracted lately and that our friendship has gotten confusing and I feel lines have blurred, so I quit the chaplaincy and decided to minister to young children in an orphanage instead.

Sam, I care for you deeply and I love you as a brother in Christ and a friend. But I think it's best if we have distance between us for a while. May God guide you in what you need to do.

Love,
Beverly

∾

Sam folded the note and put it to the side. He placed the tray with the tea and tomato soup at the foot of the bed. He found his coat hanging on a hook by his bed. He grabbed it and stuffed the note in his pocket.

He sprang out of bed and went for the door.

23

LIFT ME UP

The tempest raged on with its downpour. Sam slogged through the muddy terrain. His feet sank as he trudged on. The fir and oak trees quaked when the wind shook them. Branches cracked and fell. Sam was fortunate they didn't fall on him, at least not yet.

The rain was so intense that he couldn't really see what was around him. He lost his sense of direction. He stumbled into some trees and bushes. Sam went this way and that. Then, the earth gave way underneath. He fell back and slide down fast and far.

Massive flares emanated from the Sun. Stream of solar particles rushed through and ripped through the earth's magnetosphere.

Squadrons of gleaming silvery winged robots swarmed the stratosphere throughout the globe. They were tasked to protect the earth from excess solar radiation and carbon dioxide.

When the robots did their routine work, the major gusts of solar flares and particles jammed their sensors. Some began to fall out of the sky, while others moved on to other tasks.

Sam slid into a river. When he slid down, the earth covered him so much that he felt one with the mud. The current pulled him along. He bobbed up and down. Water went into his nose and mouth. At least he could see somewhat, and the mud washed away.

The water felt warm. But as he floated downstream, it got colder. Sam looked for something to grab onto to keep him from drowning. No luck.

The rain started to turn into snow. The trees, the riverbank on his right, and the ridge now on his left were covered. A frigid wind blew through the river. Sam's teeth chattered.

"Lord, save me!"

The river continued to force Sam along to whatever it willed. Sam wasn't bobbing up and down as much anymore. He was underwater more than above. Sam struggled to stay afloat. It felt like he lost his buoyancy.

Then, something like a giant metal claw clutched Sam. He was quickly hoisted out of the water. Sam saw the rivers, the rocks, and the trees getting smaller.

24

DETOUR

Sam gradually stopped shivering. It was warm inside the helicopter. Helicopters now didn't use rotors like in previous times. They were more stable and used something like thrusters that made them fly and something like fans insides the thruster to make them hover. This helicopter was huge.

He was on the floor of what looked like a space for cargo. There were no boxes. Instead, there were about two dozen other people on the floor too. There were a couple of families with small children. Others were men and women, ranging from young to old. They were all huddled in blankets and either drinking hot cocoa or soup.

A young man came up to Sam. He wore a black thick trench coat and gray pants. He had a blanket in his hands.

"Here you go."

Sam reached out for the blanket and took it.

"Thank you."

Sam wrapped himself. He felt more warmth and comfort.

"Would you like some hot cocoa or soup?"

"No thank you."

"Okay, let me know if you need anything else."

Sam looked up.

"Thank you, Lord!"

Those who didn't have wounds asked for a second helping of hot cocoa or soup. Sam noticed a couple of other young men and women black trench coats were treating some minor wounds on the children. The young man who helped him had a white Circle A on the back. The others did too. These were the real anarchists as Beverly educated him. They wanted liberty and equality but through peaceful means.

Sam was amazed at the size of the helicopter. He looked up and saw it had three levels. Each level had plenty of room to walk around. Sam saw a few people above going in and out of portals and walking around. There were rectangular windows in vertical positions along the walls of each level. The edges of the window were rounded.

Sam slowly looked down. He noticed a ladder on each side of the cargo area that led to the first level.

After a while, Sam felt warm enough that he took off the blanket. He stood up. His entire body throbbed in pain. He felt aches from the massive slide down into the river. He felt continued discomfort from the tussle with George. How were George and Nadine doing, Sam thought? And Beverly, what of her? What is going on?

Sam felt a blanket of anxiety cover him. Sam sank to the floor. But as the anxiety try to bury him, Sam kept his focus on God. He asked for peace and strength and help. The anxiety thinned out until it dissipated.

The same young man who gave him the blanket came back to Sam.

"Are you okay? I've seen you stand for a moment, but it looked like you fell on the floor."

"I'm fine. I just needed to refocus."

The young man nodded and started turning away. But, Sam raised his hand.

"Wait, please."

The young man turned towards Sam.

"Yes, you need something."

"What is going on out there?"

The man shook his head.

"I don't know. From what we know, it seems there's a massive, practically global superstorm that's causing widespread destruction. There was also a severe solar storm that has disrupted a lot of things. It's a mess worldwide. There's talks of succession from the United Gaia Council, because the lack of confidence. It is just chaos. Who can save us?!"

Sam asked for the Spirit to guide him on what to do next

"I don't know about what's happened or why it's happening. But I can tell you of someone who can give you peace, no matter what happens around you. It's a peace that's beyond all understanding and not of the world."

The young man just stood listening attentively to Sam. Sam wanted to get up. The young man helped him.

"Believe in the Lord Jesus and you will be saved. And it's not just you."

Sam's voice got louder.

"It's for all of us!"

Sam looked at the people sitting on the ground. They looked at him.

"God sent His Son, Jesus Christ, to tear down wall of separation between Him and us. Jesus brought to this earth a new way of doing things. He started a Kingdom or a movement more or less. It's not like the governments of this world, where they are hateful, violent, unjust, dishonest, and tyrannical. Jesus's Kingdom is one of love, peace, justice, freedom, and truth."

The people moved forward to listen to Sam, even some of the people who seemed to be aids on the helicopter listened to him.

"And unlike the empires and governments of our history where they are built off the bloodshed of other, Jesus used His own blood to create and expand His Kingdom. He used His death to destroy the wall of sin and darkness. But I don't worship a dead king. God rose Him up and now Jesus is sitting at the throne at the right hand of God as the King of the Universe. Jesus's Kingdom started thousands ago and continues today."

"What should we do?" asked the young man.

"Repent, and be baptized, every one of you, in the name of Jesus Christ. Ask for the forgiveness of your sins, and you will receive the gift of the Holy Spirit. For the promise is to you, and to your children, and to all who are far off, even as many as the Lord our God will call to Himself."

When two women with their children heard the words "promise" and "children," they moved closer toward Sam.

"How we can get this promise for our children and this gift called the Holy Spirit?" asked one of the women.

"By surrendering to the Lord Jesus, loving Him, trusting Him, and following Him. Do it His way, not yours. He loves you. When you are willing to hand over your lives completely to the Lord Jesus, He will give you His Spirit, the Spirit of God. When God dwells in your hearts, He will change you and you see His love for you and for everyone else. You will want to show that love back to God and show that love to others. Jesus is our only hope as a species to survive."

The people nodded and seemed receptive to what Sam said. They all look haggard, tired, and unsure of anything anymore. The women with the children and the young man seemed the most open to Christ. They came closer to Sam.

"Please we want to follow this Jesus you speak of," said one of the women.

"Then, follow Him," replied Sam. Sam spoke to a young woman wearing a black trench coat to see if they can land by water safely to baptize those who wanted to follow Jesus. She nodded. She called the pilots and explained why they needed to land temporarily. The pilots found a lake and an area safe enough to land.

Sam took the young man, the two women, and the children to the lake. Sam explained that baptism was a way to show them they have died to their old ways and now following Christ's ways. They were willing and ready to do this.

They step into the lake and kept going till they were waist deep in water.

"Based on your profession of faith, I baptize you in the name of Jesus Christ."

Sam baptized the young man, the two women, and the children by submerging them in water and bringing back up to the surface. Then as they climbed back onto the beach, the rest of the people in the cargo area, the young woman that got the pilots to land, one of the pilots, and some others wanted to follow Jesus and be baptized. Sam and the first group baptized the rest.

25

LIBERTY IN THE WIND

Sam and the new believers went back on the helicopter. They met and spent time together almost the entire day. They quickly learned to follow what Jesus commanded to His disciples shortly before He was crucified: love each other as He loved them. The result was, as Jesus said, people knew they belonged to Him. By this love of Christ, people joined the group of Christians, whether it was from the anarchists or the people the anarchists rescued along the way.

The Christians worked alongside the anarchists in caring for those they found amongst the global disaster. They also helped with whatever the anarchists needed.

Sam taught the group Scripture from his memory. He wasn't wired with a high intellect. Sam was considered average in intelligence by most standards. But one thing he excelled at was memorizing Scripture. Sam asked the believers if anyone would transcribe him when he spoke the Word.

The two women, Julia and Zoe, volunteered as transcribers. An elderly gentleman, Jules, and his wife, Sophia, also helped. A young man and a young woman, who were anarchists, along with a few others, helped too. Sam made it clear that what they wrote was from memory and to make a note of this in their copies. Sam instructed them to find a copy of Bible whenever possible, so that they could check what he said.

The young anarchist man, Andrew Logan, really asked Sam a lot of questions about the faith. He was a college student, and so was the young woman, Yuko Sunigh. She, Andrew, and a few other students followed their anarchist professor. They wanted to help make the world a freer and fairer place—but through peaceful means. They would speak out against those who claimed the identity of liberty and committed violence. They exposed them as agent provocateurs or people who just wanted to overthrow this government to set up their own.

Besides college students on the helicopter, there were a few families, former teachers, former public servants, and few others of all ages and walks of life—all anarchists. They were disenfranchised and agreed that the State and its mega-corporate tentacles were unjust, exploitative, and tyrannical. They worked to see its destruction but not by bullets, or even ballots (as if those did anything).

It was through ideas, alternatives, and persuasion they hoped to stab the stake through the heart of this ubiquitous vampire that had sucked the souls, lives, and blood of humanity. The anarchists' stake was a simple but effective one—withdraw consent. They argued if people withdrew their consent from the State and seek voluntary and peaceful ways of interacting with each other, people could handle themselves, and the State would crumble.

The anarchists in this giant helicopter wasn't made up of one group. Anarchists of different stripes from different communities banded together when the disaster happened. These groups already formed bonds through mutual aid, defense, and trade. Anarchism revived when the United Gaia Council became the global super state. On the helicopter, the anarchists organized as a syndicate.

"How is the government not picking us up in the sky?" asked Sam. "This is the biggest helicopter I've ever seen."

"The helicopter uses cloaking technology that makes us untraceable," replied Andrew as he sipped his chocolate.

They were sitting at a small table attached to the wall inside Andrew's quarters. They were going over Scripture. Sam had a coffee. He was learning to be a barista from the anarchists who knew their craft.

"Cloaking?"

"Yes."

Cloaking technology was used in the war before the UGC formed. Cloaking was used from large vehicles to personal overcoats known as cloakers. One of the first decrees of the government was to ban this technology. Of course, people can still get cloakers if they knew where to look.

"Wow. Say, I'd like to meet your professor you kept mentioning. What was his name...Stoneham?"

"It's Stonoam. Stonoam Stomsky. Yeah, sure. He would be happy to meet you. Besides, this might benefit you in your barista training."

Andrew and Sam finished their drinks and went to the level above them. They entered a room where a group of people sat down around a donut shaped table. The people sat on cushions. They were diverse. Men and women who were indigenous natives of South America, South Americans, Lebanese, Syrians, or Africans.

There was a man lighter than the others. He sat in the center of the table. He looked like he was of Mediterranean, Native American, and Caucasian descent. He was handsome and distinguished. He had his jet- black hair with gray stripes pulled back in a braided ponytail that ended around the middle of his back.

He was preparing some kind of drink. He put what looked like dried shriveled bits of green and brown leaves into a gourd-shaped vessel. He shook it gently and tilted the gourd slightly. The man gently inserted what looked like a metal straw. He poured a little bit of cold water through the straw. And then, the man poured hot water from a tea kettle into the gourd. He drank the contents until it was empty. He repeated the process but didn't put more leaves. This time, he passed it to someone else. That person drank whatever was in there till it was gone. And then handed back to the man. The man did the same thing as before but handed to someone else. This process just repeated. The gourd with a metal straw moved around the table and back.

The man looked and saw Sam and Andrew.

"Please join us," he said with a smile, his hand extended out to them. His tone of voice was warm and sincere.

Sam and Andrew picked up some cushions and joined the table.

As the gourd was passed again, some said Gracias or thank you to tell the man they had enough. The man refilled the gourd to give it to Andrew. After Andrew finished, it was Sam's turn.

Sam looked at the gourd and the small wisps of steam rising from it.

"Thank—"

"No, no, no," said the man gently. "If you say that, it means you don't want any. You say, 'Thank you' or 'Gracias' when you're done and don't want anymore."

"Sorry."

"No worries."

Sam drank from the straw. The drink was unlike anything he ever had. It was earthy yet smooth. His eyes lit up.

"That, my friend, is called yerba mate. It's very good stuff. Go on drink up."

"I like it!"

"Good. I'm glad." The man smiled and nodded. "I always enjoy making mate and sharing it with others. This is one of my favorites things to do in life."

Sam drank till the straw made a sucking sound. He handed it to the man to fill up more. The man got rid of the mate inside the gourd. He put them in a bin beside him, which was used for compost. He then put new mate leaves in and started the whole process again. More people drank, including Andrew and Sam.

One of the indigenous South American natives, who finished, raised his finger and began to speak. He was dressed in the garb of his tribe.

"Stonoam, since the government is in danger of breaking into pieces, should we joined those who want to secede or overthrow it?"

Stonoam, the man who made the mate, rubbed his chin.

"No," he responded as he shook his head. "Let it collapse on its own. As tyrannical the State is, we must resist the urge to join those who want revolution. History has shown what happened to our anarchist brothers and sisters before us when we threw our lot with revolutionaries."

Stonoam was referring to instances like the Russian Revolution. After the communists overthrew the Czar with the help of anarchists, they backstabbed them and killed the anarchists off.

"But Stonoam, what are we doing then? Shouldn't now be the right time to avenge the blood of my people."

The United Gaia Council turned a blind eye and even supported Dragon Corp when they took over land and killed some in this man's tribe who refused to leave.

"I understand Mutai. I really do. My parents were murdered by the State as well."

He pounded the table. He sneered.

"And as much as we want to see this infernal monster sliced up with his bones grounded up into powder and burned, we must take the high road to win hearts and minds for freedom. We are beating the State bit by bit with our ways."

"Stonoam, Mutai may have a point," chimed in a Lebanese woman. "If we join those who want to break away, we will bring this monster to a swifter end."

Stonoam shook his head.

"We may bring this monster to a swift end, Amal. But then what, we help give birth to another one. Don't you understand this by now? Revolutionaries, secessionists, and rebels are statists too. They're just not the ones in power. And rather killing the beast, they just want to take the reins of it to trample on others."

A Syrian woman sitting nearby nodded her head. "I agree Stonoam. I agree."

Sam leaned into Andrew's ear.

"What is all this," he whispered.

"These are anarchists from all over discussing what to do."

Sam was confused by the answer but didn't ask any further.

"I may be an agnostic, my friends, but I do live by this old Quaker saying," said Stonoam after he drank a cup of mate. "If, in order to defeat the beast, one has to become a beast, then bestiality has in fact won."

The other anarchists started to see to what Stonoam was saying. They nodded in agreement.

"Just because the world is in a crisis doesn't mean we should throw out patience and caution."

Stonoam looked at Sam. He stretched out his hand towards him.

"What's say you?"

"Well...umm...."

"It's okay, you're among friends."

Sam looked around the table. Everyone had their eyes on him. He gulped. He didn't know what to say. Andrew put his hand on Sam's shoulder and leaned towards his ear to whisper.

"Go for it. Speak whatever the Spirit tells you."

Sam prayed quickly in his head. He looked around and nodded.

"All right...well...I do believe that liberty and free will is inherent and natural to this Universe. It's the gift that the Creator gave to His creatures, particularly us."

The anarchists nodded to what Sam was saying.

"Since we are made in the image of our Creator, liberty, justice, and equality for all people is definitely what we should strive for," he said as looked around at those who sat at the table.

"But," Sam said as he lifted his right index finger upward. "These things cannot fully happen unless we all change our hearts. All political or economic solutions—whether statist or anarchist—are doomed to fail because they don't address the human heart."

The anarchists continued to listen. Stonoam rubbed his chin, trying to understand what this fellow was saying.

"Hmmm...," responded Stonoam.

"Now the Lord is the Spirit and where the Spirit of the Lord is, there is liberty."

When they heard liberty, they perked up, even Stonoam. Sam was standing and pacing around while facing them as he spoke.

"This liberty I'm talking about isn't merely referring to freedom in the tiddlywinks game called politics. It's something much more liberating. It's being free from evil and wickedness. These things, not institutions, have caused tyranny, oppression, and destruction. But this freedom is secure, unlike others, because it's been purchased by the Liberator King, Jesus of Nazareth. We were called to seek this freedom. But what are we to do with it? Scripture says, 'For you, brothers, were called for freedom. Only don't use your freedom for gain to the flesh, but through love be servants to one another.'

So, it's not an unbridled narcissism that some think is freedom. It's liberty to love and care each other in ways unlike this world. Love is core to this freedom. It's the very constitution of my Lord's Kingdom. Love permeates all in it. Jesus said to love God with all your heart, mind, soul, and strength, and to love your neighbor as yourself, to love your enemies..."

The anarchists were amazed at what Sam was saying. Some shook their heads and left the table, while others nodded and continued to listen.

"...And he said to his followers to love each other as Jesus loved them, so that the world would know they belong to Him. Love is the signature of those who follow Jesus completely. Why?...because God is love. He showed this to us. Unlike empires that use the blood of others as their foundation, Jesus used His own blood as a foundation to build His Kingdom. This new freedom is the call to love unconditionally."

Sam sat back down. He faced downward and closed his eyes.

"Thank you for sharing," said Stonoam. He tilted his head side-to-side and his hands up gesturing.

"These are some things to think about. Anyone else want to chime in?"

Others spoke to give their take on things or on what Sam testified in front of them. Sam asked them questions about anarchism and they in turn asked questions about the Kingdom of God. When the conversation died down, Sam asked Stonoam how to prepare mate. Stonoam gladly showed him. Those who stuck around wanted another round. This time, Sam prepared it. They drank, ate, and talked until around Midnight.

26

COLD DESCENT

"What do you mean you want to go down there?" asked Andrew. "That's crazy!"

Sam, Andrew, and the other believers were gathered together. They filled the cargo area. Some were leaning on the railings above. As much as the anarchists who weren't believers were accommodating, they didn't want to impose by taking up too much space. Instead, they decided to be crowded and uncomfortable as a good testimony to their hosts.

"It's safer to stay up here," chimed in Zoe.

Sam shook his head.

"Following Jesus isn't about creature comforts and safety. It's about following Him where He leads you to go."

Sam felt the Spirit of Christ tugging at his heart to go down to the earth to reach out to the lost and sacred. The destruction of the earth's climate continued to ravage on. Not to mention, talks of a civil war and succession continued to fester. The State was impotent to do anything about this and more people continued to lose faith in the State. The only thing they could do was become more base in their tyranny in areas they where they had the most control. Meanwhile, the mega-corporations, like Dragon Corp, got stronger and rose above the water so to speak. Dragon Corp devoured other corporate entities.

"We need you here," protested Yuko.

"No, you don't. Brothers and sisters, you don't need me. You're letting the Spirit lead you, and you're obeying Christ. You're like the Thessalonian church when one of our spiritual forefathers, Paul said '... concerning brotherly love, you have no need that one write to you. For you yourselves are taught by God to love one another'."

Sam looked around the area and up above. Sam stood in the center of the cargo area whenever he taught them.

"You honor God the Father and our Lord Jesus. You walk in the Spirit and show the love of Christ to one another. I have nothing else to teach you. I don't want you to become dependent on me but on God. I'm just a human being like the rest of you, with ailments and all."

Sam began to cry.

"Brothers and sisters, you know my condition and what I was born as, yet your love increased even more and cared for me. You have taught me more about God's love than I taught you. The only thing I can leave you with is this: hold fast to your faith in Christ and continue to mature in Him and seek Him. Otherwise, you'll slide back into the primordial ooze of sin and darkness. Don't let that happen. Seek the light, for you are children of the light."

"Well, may the Lord's will be done," said a brother.

The believers placed their hands on Sam for guidance and protection. They hugged and cried. Sam left their presence after this and went to Stonoam.

"Are you sure you want to do this?" asked Stonoam.

Sam sat at a table with Stonoam. It was same donut-shaped table from before. This time, it was just two of them drinking mate. Before then, Stonoam and all the other anarchists met up to decide whether they should land to check on their communities. They did not have any communication. They voted and came to a consensus that this was the best thing to do.

"Yes, I feel the Spirit of my God compelling me to go down."

Stonoam drank his fill from the gourd. He nodded.

"I understand you want to follow your conscience. Then, if that's the case, do what your conscience tells you. That is our natural right as human beings: to follow with our conscience without anyone or anything stopping us from doing so."

After Sam drank his fill, Stonoam spoke again.

"Is there anything you want me to do for you, friend?"

"Yes, Stonoam I do, but it's a big request. Please make sure my brothers and sisters in Christ are safe where they want to settle. They will be deciding this soon, and they will be coming to you when they do."

"Sam," said the former professor with his hand on Sam's shoulder.

"It's a very small request. They are also free to settle among us if they choose. You have been very true to what you believe and have helped us a great deal."

"Thank you, my friend," Sam replied as he nodded to accept the compliment. "You have been gracious and hospitable. Now tell me where does your conscience, or as you call it the Spirit, lead you to be dropped off?"

"Yes, here's where I need you to go," said Sam as he handed him a paper.

"Set our coordinates for the Abyss," requested Stonoam.

"The Abyss? Are you sure?" asked the pilot.

"Yes," replied Stonoam sadly.

Stonoam shed a tear.

"Sir," said the copilot. She noticed his tears and sorrow.

"No, please call me Stonoam. We have no ranks or hierarchies."

"Sorry....Stonoam, are you okay?"

"No, I'm not."

He left the control room. Stonoam went to the armory. He saw Sam.

Sam grabbed a foldable karambit. It was doubled edged and sharp enough to cut through about any metal. The anarchists got them from syndicates in a region formerly known as Indonesia. He placed it in one of his pockets.

He wore his black shirt and pants that had multiple zippers and pockets. They were made of fibers that responded to weather conditions. If it were cold, the shirt became long-sleeved and well insulated. The pants kept you warm too by becoming insulated. If it were hot, the shirt became a T-shirt and the pants became shorts. They fit snuggly around his feminine body.

He also grabbed a kukri and a Bowie knife. They were in sheaths on each of side and concealed under the black overcoat the anarchists wore. But instead of a white Circle A on the back, it had a white cross.

Yuko trained Sam on how to defend himself with a knife. She showed him anything from Eskrima to Selat.

Sam also grabbed two throwing knives and slid them in on the inside cuffs of his calf-length black leather boots. He finally grabbed a gold-plated bracelet and wore it on his wrist. It had a golden button on top. Sam pressed it. The bracelet morphed into a crossbow you can shoot from your wrist. Sam pressed the button on top of the crossbow. It transformed back into a bracelet.

"Never thought you were the type to pick up weapons," Stonoam said, startling Sam. "I thought you were pretty much a pacifist."

"I thought I wouldn't have pick up a weapon too. But where I'm going, I may need them to get through. I pray that doesn't happen. I may be arming myself, but these things can fail. God is my shield and defense."

Sam picked up another weapon that looked like a gun. He squinted one eye and peered through its sight, but he shook his head and put it away.

"First and foremost, I need to trust Him no matter what."

Stonoam put his hand on Sam's shoulder.

"Look, Sam, you don't have to do this. Just stay with us. You are free to practice your faith without any hassle."

"I appreciate the offer, Stonoam... I really do. I know I don't have to go to the Abyss."

Sam turned from Stonoam. He looked out a window nearby. He saw that they were approaching the Abyss. He could see that a blizzard pounded where he would make his beachhead. Sam turned back towards Stonoam and crossed his arms. His hands rubbed his arms a couple of times.

"But I must! I feel that my God is leading me. I also need to find someone I deeply care about to make sure she's okay. I feel that she's also somewhere in the Abyss."

"Ohh....I see," Stonoam said smiling as he rubbed his beard. He usually didn't have facial hair, but he recently let it grow.

"What's her name?"

Sam was about to tell him, but they got interrupted.

"Stonoam, we got trouble," said someone over Stonoam's communicator.

"What is it?"

"We got government fighter bots circling around."

"So?"

"So?! They're trying to destroy our cloak!"

"How do you know?"

"We detected the bot using decryption algorithms on us. We're holding them off but don't know for how long."

Stonoam looked at Sam.

"I can't let you go down. It's too dangerous."

"No," protested Sam. "I will save your life and everyone else's on this helicopter if you send me down. I will be the distraction to them while you escape."

"That's suicide!"

"No, that's love."

Sam and Stonoam quickly went to a bay that launched out escape pods. Sam jumped into one. He was about to close the hatch, but Stonoam's hand stopped him.

"Sam, may your God keep you safe. Good luck!"

"Thank you. Following Jesus isn't for those who love themselves more than others."

Sam closed the hatch. Stonoam launched the pod. It shot out with a fierce velocity. The fighter bots started to pursue Sam.

"If you exist," Stonoam looked out below, "may you keep Sam safe. He's a good man."

Stonoam spoke into his communicator.

"Let's get out of here!"

The fighter bots opened fire but missed.

"Come and get me!" Sam screamed.

They fired again. This time, they hit the pod. The pod shattered.

The fighter bots circled around to find any signs of life. Once their sensors returned a negative signal for life, they gave up and flew to another part of the sky. Below them, Sam was lying on the snowy beach, face down.

27

FLURRY

Snow blasted through the gusts of wind. The wind howled. The ocean roared. The snow descended onto Sam and buried him. He was soon a big white lump on the beach.

The symphony from the forces of nature played on till it faded into the ether. But the ocean carried on with a solo. The waves crashed against the beach with the water reaching towards the lump of snow. The waves crashed again, and the water was now covering a part of the lump that was facing the ocean.

The wind howled again. It blew the snow towards the ocean.

After some time passed, footsteps crunched over the snow-covered sand. The footsteps headed towards the lump. A man walked around the snowy bump, kicked it a bit, and knelt down by the part that blanketed Sam's upper body. With his gloved hand, he dove into the snow. To his surprise, he felt a grip and tug underneath.

"Thank you," Sam said after he sipped some coffee.

"Don't mention it," said the man who pulled him out of the snow.

The man scooped coffee out of a pot with a metal ladle and poured it into his earthenware cup. Sam also had the same type of cup. He rested the ladle against the pot's handle that was hooked onto a metal stand, hanging over a makeshift hearth.

The fire from the hearth, as well as the coffee, kept Sam and the man warm inside the small cave. The cave's interior was shaped like a dome. They were sitting on rocks opposite to each other with the hearth between them.

"Sorry if the coffee isn't that good," said the man.

"No, it's good. It really is. I prepare coffee myself and this is really good. So, thank you."

"You're welcome."

He was a young man in his late twenties. He looked as if he was of North African descent. He had a small but thick beard. He rubbed his beard a bit after he drank a few sips.

"It keeps me warm," said the man. "You should grow one to keep your face warm."

"I can't."

"Ohh...sorry. My name's Majid," he said as he put his hand out.

"Sam. It's a pleasure to meet you," he said as he shook Majid's hand.

"Likewise, my friend.... likewise."

Sam noticed an old tattered book resting on a rock behind Majid.

"Is that a Quran?"

Majid hesitated to answer but finally gave a response.

"Yes...yes, it is."

"Okay, I'm a person of the Book."

Sam meant that he followed the Bible.

"I see. Would you like more coffee?"

"Yes, please. Thank you for your kindness, Majid."

"Thank God, Sam," he said as he pointed upward. "He kept you safe."

"Yes, He did. Thank you, God."

Sam looked upward.

"I saw your pod destroyed by the fighter bots. I saw you fall out. How did you not got get finished off by them?"

"I don't know Majid, it was God, ultimately."

"What brings you here, Sam?"

"I'm here to preach the message the Greatest Prophet and Word of God, Jesus Christ, has for humanity. It is to turn from their sinful ways and submit to God, who is all-loving, merciful, and just."

"Yes, He is my friend. Yes, He is."

"But unfortunately, I can't say it's the only reason. I'm looking for a friend to make sure she's safe."

Majid nodded his head.

"That explains why you're armed."

Majid was armed with knives as well. And the rod he used to trudge through snow was wooden on the outside but metal on the inside, so he could use it for protection.

"Sam, you are very wise in taking such precautions in the Abyss. Do you know where she's at?"

"No, but I know she's here. How far in, I don't know."

"Which is why you're not going," said a familiar voice behind them. Majid's eyes widened. Sam turned around.

"Elmira?!"

Elmira stood at the mouth of the cave. She wore a dusty brown leather overcoat, which was now covered in snow. There was a belt of the same color hanging from waist, leaving the coat open. Underneath, Elmira wore a black uniform of some kind. It looked metallic in texture. There was also some kind of scarlet design over the uniform. Neither Sam nor Majid could make out what it was.

She held a giant rod. One end of it was resting on the snowy, sandy ground. Elmira picked up the rod and entered the cave. Her demeanor was different. Rather than the warm and hospitable like she was at her cabin, she was now cold and clinical. Her voice also matched her new countenance.

"How did find me?"

Elmira didn't respond.

"Sam, you cannot do this. I will not let you find Beverly nor let you spread your poison."

Majid wasn't sure what to do. He didn't want to get involved get this conflict. He wanted to flee, but he felt it would be unwise to do so.

Sam tapped his chin a couple of times to think of what to say.

"Elmira, why are you acting like this?"

She didn't answer the question.

"You will not destroy humanity with your dangerous ways, and you will not propagate anymore imperfections. We cannot allow this. Humanity is on the cusp of a new stage as a species."

"You know what I think," responded Sam. Sam stood up.

Elmira didn't regard his comment.

"You're not who you say are."

Elmira remained silent. She just analyzed him taking some small paces around the cave.

"I think that letter you gave me was a forgery."

"Sam, we cannot allow you to regress humanity into superstition. Humanity's survival depends on it."

"Where's Beverly, Elmira! If that's your name! And who is this 'we' you keep referring to?"

"This is your last warning. Come with me and this will be resolved."

"Majid, get out of here while still you can," ordered Sam as he kept his eyes on Elmira. "You don't need to worry about this."

Majid went for the opening, but Elmira tripped Majid with her rod. He hit his head against the wall of the cave. The fall gashed the right side of his forehead.

"You are not going anywhere till further notice. We will deal with you and your kind later."

"Sam Lysander, what is it going to be? Shall you come peacefully?"

"You don't answer any of my questions, so why should answer yours?"

"I will take that as a no."

Elmira lifted the rod to whack Sam. Sam leapt back. Her rod crashed into the pot on the hearth. The pot flew and the coffee splattered. Sam ran over to Majid and get him so they could escape. She speared Sam and pinned him against the wall. Elmira slid him upward by his manubrium. Sam dangled in excruciating pain. She held him up with one hand on the rod.

The fire in the hearth was burning. From the fire, Sam noticed an inhuman gleam in Elmira's eyes.

"Sam!" yelled Majid. "Here!"

Majid threw his rod, so Sam could catch it. Elmira swatted it out of the air. She quickly turned her head to face Majid. Her arm extended several feet and clutched Majid's throat. She pinned him against the wall too. Elmira confirmed what Sam thought. He pulled out his kukri and sliced the rod in two. Sam fell and rolled.

Elmira snapped her head back towards Sam. Sam shot a small, serrated arrow from his wrist crossbow into her left eye while he was on the ground. Her head jerked upward. She lost her grip on Majid. He fell on his butt.

Crackles, sizzles, and sparks came from the hit. The arrow pierced through her head and protruded on the other side. Elmira pulled the arrow out and tossed it. She looked at Sam.

"Agggghhhh!" screamed Majid. He shook. He couldn't run. He was paralyzed with fear.

Sam saw the gaping hole on her face. He saw the damaged circuits and severed wires.

Her hand became like a sword and made a chopping motion towards Sam. He guarded himself with his crossbow. She destroyed it, but fortunately, Sam wasn't harmed. Sam went for his bowie knife, but Elmira stomped on his wrist with her right foot to pin it against the ground. Elmira shook her head in disapproval. She smiled in glee. Her left hand morphed into the sword. She was ready to stab Sam.

"Noooo!" yelled a woman, who was at the mouth of the cave. She threw a small javelin at Elmira. The javelin split into three smaller ones in midair. They pierced Elmira in three places: the head, the middle of the back, and between her butt. Elmira fell on her knees. Sam moved out of the way, so she could fall facedown.

Sam got up and went over to Majid to make sure he's okay. They both looked in disbelief.

28

REDUX

"Sam?"

Sam and Majid just looked at the woman. They were apprehensive of who to trust.

"Sam."

"El—Elmira?"

Elmira went over to Sam and Majid. They moved back in fear. Sam nor Majid were sure if this was Elmira or another android trying to kill them. They weren't even sure if there was such a woman named Elmira. But Sam noted that her mannerisms were the same as at the cabin.

She looked at the electronic duplicate of herself. She gasped. She cried.

"Oh, honey! I'm sorry."

Elmira hugged both Sam and Majid.

"It's okay. You're safe now. I'm the real Elmira."

She got up and reexamined the robotic knockoff of her. Sam noticed she wore a black overcoat that had a white Circle A on the back. Elmira was an anarchist. Sam wondered if Stonoam sent her.

Elmira turned over the android with her foot. She also used her foot to open the brown overcoat. Elmira revealed scarlet a seven-headed, ten-horned dragon.

"It's just as I thought," she said in disgust. She spat on the dead droid. "Dragon Corp!"

"Dragon Corp?! What do they have to do with this?" Sam asked. "And how did you know to find us here?"

Sam got up. He became skeptical of Elmira again.

"I don't know, but they are after my daughter. All I know is that I escaped after this thing trapped me at the cabin, shortly after you left. I tracked it down before it could harm Beverly."

"So why did it come to me instead."

Sam still wasn't sure what to believe. Majid wasn't sure of anything anymore.

"I don't know why ... maybe it tracked you down to draw Beverly out. They know you are associated with her. The surveillance bots gathered information on everyone. That's why I tried to get away from them by living in the wilderness."

Sam was confused now. Why Beverly? What did the Dragon Corporation want with her?

Elmira picked up the kukri. She toyed with it a bit and looked at Sam and Majid.

"I understand your feelings. It's mutual. I'm a little skeptical of you too."

"What?!" exclaimed Sam. "I would never hurt Beverly. I love and care about her. I made this journey here to make sure she's okay. I would lay my life down for her."

"I know," she said as she handed the kukri back to him. She took his hands and knelt before him. She wept.

"Please go find her. Protect her. Escape together away from danger. Stay away from everyone you know...including me. Just please...please...no more dangerous stuff. Practice your faith with her in secret. Marry her. Love her. You have my blessing. You just have to keep her safe!"

Tears flowed onto his hands. He lifted her up. Sam wiped away the tears.

"Don't worry. I'll do everything I can to keep her safe. But while I'm looking for her, I must also show the Light of Christ to others in the Abyss."

Sam embraced Elmira. She pulled back.

"But what about..."

"Don't worry. I will find her or die trying."

The wind blew frigid gusts outside. The cave became colder. Elmira helped Majid and Sam put the hearth back together. Elmira threw some powder onto the wood and ignited in a flame. The fire from earlier burned out.

"What do we with this?" asked Majid, referring to the wannabe Elmira.

The real Elmira pulled out a vial from her bag she carried. She sprinkled another kind of powder over the android. Within a couple of minutes, it became a foamy substance and dissolved.

The three sat around the hearth and had broth this time. They talked a bit. The blizzard resurged, so they remained in the cave and rested by the warm fire until it died down.

29

GATEWAY OF THE ABYSS

Sam, Majid, and Elmira hiked out little ways on the beach. They looked towards the interior of the Abyss. Ahead of them was an abandoned boardwalk. Before the war and UGC, it was a long-standing major coastal attraction that lasted for centuries. But now, it lies in ruins. Sections of the huge wooden roller coaster on the boardwalk collapsed. The entire structure rotted in decay.

The wind picked up again. Some sandy snow blew around. The wind howled but it wasn't as loud. It nipped at their ears and noses. The wind stung a bit, but it was bearable. All three just stood there for a while looking at the boardwalk.

"You want us to come with you?" asked Majid.

Sam shook his head.

"I need to do this alone. I don't want to put any of you in danger."

"Sam," Elmira said as she put her gloved hand on his shoulder. He turned towards her.

"If you find Beverly, tell her I love her and to be happy."

"Okay." Sam nodded. He embraced her. "Take care, Elmira."

Tears welled up in his eyes. Elmira's eyes also poured out tears.

"You too, Sam. I love you."

"I love you too."

He kissed her cheek.

"Sam," said Majid with his hand on Sam's other shoulder. "Take care, my friend." He gave Sam a hug.

"You too, Majid."

"May God keep you safe."

"May God keep you safe as well."

They stopped hugging. Sam looked onward.

"One more thing, Sam, Nietzsche's saying is true here: 'If you gaze too long into an abyss, the abyss will gaze back into you.' So please be aware of this as venture into the Abyss."

"Thanks again, my friend" replied Sam as he looked back at Majid. "I'll remember that."

Sam gave them nods and turn towards the boardwalk. He trudged forward heading for the Gateway into the Abyss.

30

THE LIGHT IN THE ABYSS

Crunch...crunch...crunch. Creak...creak...creak.

Sam climbed the wooden stairs that led up to the boardwalk. He looked in awe at the rickety remains of the giant rollercoaster. He never had been on a rollercoaster. It was one of the relics from the past that he only heard of.

The Abyss recently became a prison land for those who actively rebelled against the UGC and the new society. Since the UGC supposedly abolished the death penalty, they carved out lands to put those who were considered treasonous or unable to conform. These were areas that were already considered ungovernable. So, it made sense for the UGC to wall these areas off and make them prisons. The Abyss was in that category. They called it the Abyss because whoever went in never came out.

Shortly before the superstorm, the UGC started rounding up anarchists and others, including some Christians and Muslims, and put them in the Abyss and similar areas. Eron C. Aesar pushed for Dragon Corp to conduct an extensive risk management project for the government on those who wouldn't accept the new ways of Gaia or the transhuman ethos. (Eron preached for transhumanism. He was becoming a premier evangelist for it.) Rather than trying to contain these nonconformists in society, it was far easier to exile them into these regions. The frontiers of these areas were guarded by fighter bots and heavy armed police. But one could get out if they renounce their ways and committed to rejoining society. But this plan halted when the climate radically altered. And now people here were just living their life.

The government was still broken down from the disasters. They were trying to restore order but ineffective in doing so. Talks of succession or civil war were widespread because of their exile policy and an utter loss of faith in the State, but no real action yet.

Sam also saw the other artifacts known as rides. One that looked like an elliptical train track, which was on a raised angled platform, had frosted weeds growing over it. The cars that seemed to go on the track were flipped upside down on the ground. Next to this ride was a giant Ferris wheel. Despite its age, it was in a good shape. The seats were filled with snow and the wheel was encased in white. But, the swing ride nearby wasn't so lucky. It was broken in two. The upper part with the swings attached collapsed onto the roof of another ride. This ride had pictures of old timey musicians and old cars that seemed like they would move in a circular, angled motion.

The wind shear stung Sam's cheeks. Snow pelted him occasionally. He started to explore more of the ancient coastal attraction.

The windows of the arcades were smashed in. The machines were rusted out and either turned over or busted up. Dried up seaweed and sand covered most of them. The boutiques and concession stands were boarded up. The snack and coffee carts were kicked over and covered in frozen barnacles. It looked like at some point the ocean flooded the boardwalk. Maybe it was when the sea levels rose dramatically.

This was the one thing that Sam was grateful for the United Gaia Council. It aggressively tried to combat the effects of climate change. But, at what price? And the geo-engineering robots were really just a band aid to a bigger problem. Maybe they actually made the global climate worse by trying to control everything. From what he had seen and experienced on the helicopter, the weather around the globe was unstable. And what if the climate change was natural not a reaction to human destruction? These thoughts swirled in Sam's head as he slowly walked around the ruins from a different world.

He tried to picture a time when people—men, women, children, families—enjoyed this boardwalk. He tried to imagine people on rides screaming and enjoying the thrill. People eating whatever food and drink they bought, savoring each bite or sip while sitting down on the benches or having fun on the beach, playing and basking in the sun. And swimming or surfing the waves. His reverie vanished when Sam noticed something.

He saw scrawling and art on some boarded-up windows and walls. From what he gathered, they seemed to be done by Nihils. Sam now treaded with caution. But Sam couldn't help but be drawn to some of the art he saw. Some of them were insightful, interesting, and beautifully done. One in particular was a mural of the cosmos. It was drawn so it moved along the way he was going; it was taking a bird's eye view of the Universe.

It started with the beautiful rendering of earth, then it was the solar system, including the minor planets. Each phase of the mural was well-rendered. Then, it zoomed out to the Milky Way. The perspective of the mural seemed to shift to a seemingly more panoramic view. It showed the Andromeda Galaxy and nebulas like the Horsehead, Crab, Cat's Eye, and the Pillars of Creation of the Eagle Nebula. The mural culminated into a black space filled with other galaxies, nebulas, and quasars. At the top of mural, a statement written in white across the entire span of it read: NOTHING IS THE TRUTH. AND THE TRUTH SHALL SET YOU FREE! The N at the beginning was backwards. It had also a circle around it.

Sam ventured further. He noticed another scrawling that read: DESTROY YOUR ILLUSIONS! AND YOU WILL FREE YOUR MIND! Sam noticed another scrawling over a picture of chains over the world. It read: BRAKE THE CHAINS OF THIS WORLD TO BE FREE!

Sam saw some more of their philosophy written over the sign and the wall of a boarded-up coffee house. TO HAVE NO PURPOSE IS TO HAVE ONE. BUT TO HAVE A PURPOSE IS TO HAVE NONE! GOING SOMEWHERE IS GOING NOWHERE. BUT GOING NOWHERE IS GOING SOMEWHERE!

Sam went further to what seemed to be the center of the boardwalk. There was a stone image of the Angel of Death. At the bottom of the statue, it read: BETTER TO BE DEAD THAN TO BE ALIVE! TO BE DEAD IS TO BE FREE!

Just as Sam finished reading this, he heard an unworldly screech from above!

Bats?! At least, these creatures had the wings of a bat. They acted like them too. These beings slept upside down on the wooden beams of the giant roller coaster. But their appearance was not quite like a bat. They looked similar to the Angel of Death, also known as the Grim Reaper. Their screech didn't sound like a bat; it was somewhere between a howl of a wolf and the scream of an owl. In their skeletal hands, they held scythes. The blades on them resembled the talons of an eagle. And they swooped towards Sam.

Sam pulled out his kukri and his Bowie. Sam sliced at several descendants of Death. He dodged their hacks and countered with his own. No blood flowed from Sam's cuts. Instead, sparks and sizzles came from the wounds. When Sam saw they were machines, he intensified his attack. At least six fell and crashed onto the ground.

More oncoming squads of these ghastly machines descended onto Sam. Sam swung and sliced into two, either vertically or horizontally. He successfully destroyed them as they attacked. But Sam's stamina waned. For a brief moment, he had a respite. From the other side of the park, he saw more flying towards him. Sam looked for a place to hide.

He saw an old cafe. Fortunately, it wasn't boarded up and there were no windows, just a door. Sam dashed for it and shut the door behind him, locking it. Sam quickly found tables, chairs, and whatever was heavy enough to barricade the door.

Sam heard the pounding and hacking against the door, along with screeches. The barricade would hold them off but not for long.

Sam scrambled to the kitchen area. It was dark and littered with pots and pans. Sam crashed into them and stumbled onto the floor. Sam grabbed the handles of the kitchen drawer to lift himself up. He looked for another room to hide or a back exit to escape. Nowhere to go!

The death machines hacked through the door and smashed the barricades. They swarmed the cafe and the kitchen.

These merciless machines ascended out of the cafe after a few minutes. They exited the same way they entered. The shrills and screeches faded after they perched themselves on the beams of the roller coasters. They resumed their slumber. Now there was silence in the Abyss.

It was nightfall. There was no snow tonight. The wind howled throughout the old boardwalk.

Somewhere between the Angel of Death statue and the boarded-up cafe, there was an old oil drum that once served as a trash can. Tonight, it had flames ascending from it. They crackled. Nihils were gathered around the fire. Men, women, children, young, old, danced to music. With the exception of a few voices, they moved in silence. Those who were speaking were sitting at the old decrepit benches and eating.

They listened to Depeche Mode. They just finished listening to "Embrace the Silence." Then, momentary silence followed by "The Policy of Truth."

The Nihils stepped it up a bit. Even those sitting down moved to the song. As the song progressed, they danced vigorously to it, especially every time they heard the chorus. The Nihils gave themselves over to a state of euphoria to the song's lyrics, riffs, and rhythms.

When the synth riff interlude played, the doors of the ruined cafe flung open. They didn't notice at first. But when a few did, they all stopped dancing.

They froze in amazement. The only ones that continued with the rumpus were Depeche Mode.

The Nihils quaked in fear but were too paralyzed in fear to run. There before them stood the Angel of Death. It held in its bony hand a huge, razor-sharp sickle. In the other, it held a cup of coffee, with steam emanating from it. When the Nihils saw this, their fears dissipated into the air too.

Making and offering coffee to Nihils was a sign of peace and goodwill. They stood in reverence to the Angel of Death. They bowed before it, but the Angel shook his head. The sickle vanished, so his hand could be free. He signaled with his hand for them to get up.

The Angel of Death went over to a young Nihil girl and handed the coffee to her. She nodded in respect. The song ended. Everything was silent, except for the crackle of flames from the trash can.

Angel of Death projected something in the air. It looked like a cross. The Angel of Death faced the cross and knelt before it one knee. His head bowed and skeleton hands clasped together.

The Nihils were shocked by this gesture. Why would the Angel of Death, the archetypal figure of who they are, submit before a cross?

The Angel of Death faced the Nihils.

"I bowed because I have been defeated," he spoke. His voice sounded surprisingly human. It was cold but not evil.

"One day, I will be destroyed. And it is for your benefit that I will be gone. The One who defeated me did it for you because He loved you. He was killed for you, so you may experience the freedom we all yearn for. And the real love and meaning we all seek. Yes, this system has no value or purpose, and it is destined to be destroyed. You are right in rejecting it as nonsensical. And we would be absolutely right if this Universe was empty and cold. But our freedom isn't in nothingness. Our freedom is being free from our failings, darkness, and evil and following the One who has defeated me. He will fill your hearts with His Spirit. Our joy...forget happiness. We know it's meaningless because it's fleeting. Our joy isn't in death. It's spending your lives forever with this One who loves you and is with each of you."

The Nihils continued to listen. The Angel of Death nodded at the little girl to drink the coffee. She took a sip and she passed it others to do the same.

The Angel of Death brought forth a few decanters so that others can drink too.

"If you submit your lives to Him, you spend eternity with Him. He will raise you from the dead when He returns. His system is radically different than this world's. His ways are of love, kindness, peace, truth, and justice."

The Nihils continued to pass the cup and get more coffee when they ran out. It was the best coffee they ever had.

"When He returns disease, hate, war, greed, evil, suffering, disease, and even death will be incinerated. Yes, I will be gone. But I'm not a part of the real order. The life from this One is the real order of things. Who is this One?"

The cross was still in the air.

"His name," the voice became warm, "is Jesus of Nazareth."

The Angel of Death vanished. The Cross vanished as well. Sam stood before them instead. He had three red lines painted above and three red lines below his right eye. The Nihils had the same. These lines were the marks of true Nihils. The ones Sam encountered at the church didn't have them. The red paint covered the etched-in scars of these lines. These lines represented three things: birth, life, and death. It was the cycle of the Universe for the Nihils.

He also stood before them naked. They had seen his body, but they didn't balk at him. They accepted hermaphrodites as a part of nature. Sam was freezing but he stood naked to show that he was genuine and honest. Nihils used nakedness to show they are not lying because they are being vulnerable with others.

A Nihil woman offered Sam a trench coat to keep him warm, showing she accepted his honesty. Sam appreciated her gesture.

"Sam Lysander?" asked a Nihil.

"Yes, I am."

"You're—you're the Angel of Death incarnate."

"Was. I am no longer." What they had seen was Sam's soul data.

They bowed their heads in honor to him.

"Please bow to Jesus Christ instead. For he experienced death but was risen back to the life. He has broken the cycle of nature, should I say restored it."

The Nihils were silent.

"My soul reveled in death, but Jesus's Spirit gave it life. And you too can have this life if you follow Him."

"But you taught us to reject these illusions to alleviate humanity's emptiness in this Universe," someone replied.

"Yes, I know," responded Sam.

Sam coalesced ideas together into what would become the Nihil subculture. Sam never took credit for creating it. He would only say he tied philosophies together from people from different times that were united by one glue: Nihilism.

"But I was wrong. I used our ways to foment my anger against the One who made us all. It was all because I was made this way."

Sam waved his hand up and down to show he was talking about his body.

"For that, I am sorry I've led you down the same road. I realized that God wasn't cruel and didn't make a mistake. He loves me and loves you too. He showed that to the world through His son. His son, Jesus, went to the nothingness of death, but God brought Him back from it. We have hope and love, that is our freedom; it's not death and suffering. God made us this way for own reason and for that I am grateful. I don't know what it is, but He made me this way and He loves me. He did the same for you too. Embrace His love and the life He has for you."

The Nihils didn't seem receptive. They said nothing. Just silence.

"Thank you for listening and your kindness. I'll just get my things and go."

Sam turned from them and headed back inside to get dressed. Sam left the coat that one of the Nihils gave to him in the kitchen. He suited up and tucked in his knives and headed outside.

He saw the Nihils just standing there. Sam looked at them.

"I'm glad I was able to see my people again. I don't regret it, but I must get going."

Some of the Nihils murmured amongst themselves. Sam resumed his trek into the unknown.

"Wait! Don't go O Angel of Death. Tell us about this life and light of Jesus Christ."

Sam turned around and came back to them.

31

GAZING AT THE JACKALS

Months have gone by since that day; Sam spent his days teaching them the ways of Christ. Virtually, every Nihil in this community became followers of Christ.

They didn't become followers to assimilate to the mainstream culture like some people groups in the past who were exposed to the Gospel. Nor, did Sam ever once suggest it. As a matter of fact, if they ever asked him about ditching their garb and ways, he would emphatically say no. Sam would affirm they are correct in rejecting the mainstream. Sam was showing a different way to be countercultural.

The Nihils retained some of their nihilism but they no longer believed that nothingness was the end run for the living. They contrasted their beliefs with the light, love, and life of Jesus Christ and His Kingdom. They came up with a new saying: "The Light has met the darkness, and the darkness became the light."

Some of them were zealous in going out to the other Nihil communities throughout the world to reach out to them. Sam was hesitant in sending them out yet, but he eagerly helped them get ready to undertake this endeavor.

Sam would further step back from the groups when they became more like Christ. He wasn't interested in being their go-to guy for God. Sam made it clear he could be wrong on some things.

As for baptisms, Sam didn't immerse them in water in this case. It was too frigid. He laid hands on them instead and they would become filled with the Holy Spirit.

They restored the abandoned boardwalk to the best of their abilities. The decrepit boarded-up buildings became places of life and joy. They opened up the boardwalk to the Undesirables and other exiles living in the Abyss.

Sam looked towards the dark mountains east of the boardwalk. A Nihil came up to him. He brought Sam some coffee.

"Thank you, Django," Sam said as he sipped the hot ebony brew. The aroma of the coffee invigorated his olfactory senses.

Django was a young teenage boy. He was a recent exile to the Abyss after his parents disowned him and turned him over to the State. Django became a follower of Christ the day Sam preached. Sam took him under his wing ever since.

Sam gave the coffee cup to Django so he could drink it.

"Thank you, Sam," he said after he took his drink. "I noticed you have been staring at the mountains quite a bit lately. Why?"

Sam rubbed his chin for a bit.

"I wonder what's in those mountains and beyond."

"It's the Lair of the Jackals," said a woman behind them. She was an older woman, probably in her late forties or early fifties. Despite her age, she was still wiry. She lost her family when the UGC forced them here. They died in the transport. She was still a nihilist but was also open to Christ.

"Yuna," replied Sam. "What brings you here?"

"I come here often to dream of life outside the Abyss. Why do you want to go to the Lair of the Jackals?"

"I must find Beverly. I need to know if she's still alive. I feel like she is out there further in the Abyss. I tried to shake it off, but I can't. The Abyss is a huge place. I would also love a chance to preach the message of hope to the Jackals."

"You're going to need a lot more than hope to get through to the Jackals."

"I'm aware of that," Sam responded as he revealed the knives under his black coat. He also pulled up his pants legs to show the throwing knives.

"But more so, I'm not afraid because I trust in my Lord's protection. Even if I die, I don't fear death because Jesus will raise me up when he returns. I don't care what happens to me. I just want to make sure Beverly is safe."

"Neither do I; I don't fear death either," responded Yuna. "If I die, I die. Whatever, don't care. I have nothing to live for, so I'm going with you."

"Me too," said Django.

"You're not going," replied Sam.

"What?!"

"It's too dangerous, Django."

"I'm not afraid to die either."

"Django, stay here. This community has embraced you as family and you are growing in the faith. You have so much to look forward to."

"Sam," retorted Django, "Doesn't Jesus say, 'If anyone desires to come after me, let him deny himself, and take up his cross, and follow me. For whoever desires to save his life will lose it, and whoever will lose his life for my sake will find it.' "

Sam shook his head.

"There's a difference in this case."

"How so?"

32

A DEN OF JACKALS

A couple of more months went by. The Nihils started going out of the Abyss to preach the Gospel and reach out to the other Nihil communities. They used an underground river that led out to the ocean. The Nihils built submarines coated with cloakers. The Nihils inside would also wear cloakers as a precaution against the squadrons of the fighter bots. But they had to go quickly because the fighter bots would break through cloakers eventually. Some Nihils met their watery doom already. But despite this, they felt the risk was worth it.

Sam and Nihils gathered around a fire at night. It was at the same place where Sam and the Nihils met the first time when he preached the Gospel.

"My people," said Sam as he stood by the fire.

"When I became the Angel of Death, it was to take out my vengeance on this world and on our God, but the Lord Jesus graciously showed me that He loved me in spite of my hate for Him. I was broken and renewed by His Spirit. I came to the Abyss to preach the light and love of God to you. And you have showed it to each other. There's no need for me to teach you anymore."

The Nihils looked at other and wondered where he was going with this.

"I'm plunging further into the Abyss."

The Nihils murmured amongst themselves.

"Where are you to going?" asked one of them.

"The Lair of Jackals."

"What," said several of them.

"That's crazy," said some others.

"Yes, and we're going with Sam," Yuna replied.

She and Django walked up by Sam and stood beside him.

"And we're leaving tonight," declared Django.

"You'll be killed," objected a Nihil.

"What's the difference going to the Lair of the Jackals and going out to the ocean," refuted Django.

"When you will be back?" asked another Nihil.

"I don't know," admitted Sam. "It's possible I may see you never again and these two are willing to help me as much I need it. Lord willing, they return. I must find my best friend to make sure she's okay. I must also proclaim the name of Christ to the Jackals. Lord willing, I will return."

The Nihils hugged them and wept. They laid their hands on them and said a prayer for all three. Shortly, Sam, Yuna, and Django gathered their things and ventured outside the gates of the boardwalk. They walked down the dark streets of the decaying coastal town. The only light came from the full moon. He glanced at it.

Sam pondered at what Majid meant when said before about if you gaze into the Abyss, it will gaze back at you. The three continued silently with their nocturnal trek.

The three cautiously strode through the streets. Buildings and houses were boarded up and some of the windows were smashed. Some vehicles parked on the curbs were rusted out. Others had their doors taken off or had fractured windows. Surprisingly, there were a few vehicles that were in good shape.

"We need to use lights. It's too dark," Django.

"No," replied Yuna. "We'll attract the Jackals."

"Where is everyone," whispered Sam. "Don't we have people come to the boardwalk?"

"They live on the streets very close to it," Yuna replied. "They also live really close to the coastal cliffs. The Jackals don't go to either place because they fear the fighter bots. Ever since the UGC has cordoned off our community as a prison and stuck the Jackals here, it's been unsafe. People had to leave their homes. The Jackals only come out at night."

"Figures," Sam said as he shook his head. "Whatever the UGC touches, it becomes ruined."

A howl pierced through the night air. It came from a rooftop nearby.

"The Jackals!" Django exclaimed.

"Hurry," Yuna commanded. "We must get inside somewhere."

They heard several howls, followed by growls. Sam, Yuna, and Django tried get into several houses or buildings but couldn't the boards off.

"Damn it!" yelled Sam as he punched a board he couldn't get off.

"What are we going to do?" Yuna asked.

"We're going to have to defend ourselves, but we need to find cover." Sam pulled out his Bowie knife. Yuna pulled out her pistols.

"Here," she said as gave Django one.

"I don't know how to use a gun!"

"You do now. Just point and squeeze."

"Hurry," said Sam.

They ran through the street. The Jackals leapt from rooftop to rooftop in pursuit. As Sam, Django, and Yuna continued to dash through town, the number of Jackals increased. Their howls and growls got louder and closer by the moment.

"This way!" yelled Sam.

The three turned a corner and ran down an alleyway. They could hear the Jackals screaming from above. Sam wondered when they would pounce on them.

"Look out!" yelled Yuna.

A robotic jackal leapt down towards Sam. Sam evaded the diving attacker. Yuna shot the jackal. The shot ripped a hole through it and the jackal collapsed with an electronic hiss.

Then another robotic jackal took a leap at them.

"No!" screamed Django.

This one pounced towards Yuna. Django fumbled with the gun but pulled the trigger at the last minute. It also fell with a sizzle, just inches before Yuna.

"Thanks, Kid."

Sam sprinted down the alleyway but halted violently.

"Nooo!"

"What is it," yelled Yuna.

"Dead end!"

"Help!"

"Django!"

A circle of Jackals surrounded Django. They licked their lips as they held their maces, axes, and spears.

"Leave me alone!" screamed Django as he held the gun, which trembled in his hand.

"Ha, ha, ha," mocked one of them as he swatted Django's hand with a mace.

The gun flew and it shattered as it hit the side of a building.

Django's hand was slightly lacerated from the blow. When the Jackals saw the blood trickling from his hand, they howled, and their bloodlust intensified.

"Feast," declared one.

"Nooo!" screamed Yuna. She opened fire and shot several of them in the head and chest. The circle dispersed. She shot the fleeing Jackals. They all collapsed face forward in pools of blood.

"Die, you bastards! Die!"

Django cried. Yuna went over to Django. He froze in fear.

"Are you alright," she asked as she extended her hand toward him.

Django said nothing. He just stood there. Yuna heard a grunt a little ways from them. It was a Jackal trying to crawl away. His jackal garb fell off. What they saw was an emaciated man, struggling to get away. He was bald and sickly.

Yuna lunged at him.

"Ahhh!" he screamed as she flipped him over with her foot. He landed on his back and shook in fear.

"Please don't kill me," pleaded the Jackal. "My family is starving, and I need to feed them. Please."

The Jackal burst into tears. He tried to shield himself with his trembling, bloodied hands from Yuna's cold gaze.

"Please. Don't. Let me get back to my family."

Yuna said nothing. She just gazed on. Sam wasn't sure what was going on. He was a good distance from Yuna, Django, and the Jackal.

The Jackals halted their nocturnal hunt for flesh to see at what Yuna would do.

"Please," pleaded the injured man.

Yuna said nothing. She turned from him. She walked a couple of steps away.

"Yuna, no," pleaded Django.

"Yuna, stop," protested Sam.

Yuna spun around and plunged a spear right into the man's heart. Her eyes widen and her face morphed into that of a raving lunatic or that of a Jackal when one devours flesh.

"Lord Jesus, Son of the Eternal God, have mercy on me, this woman, and my family," he screamed. Blood gushed out of his mouth.

His head turned to one side and his eyes were wide open. Tears flowed from them. He was dead.

The Jackals roared and swarmed towards Yuna and Django.

"Nooo!" screamed Django.

A spear pierced through Yuna's back and the serrated tip poked out from her belly.

Her crazed look gave away to fear, dread, and regret. Then an axe sliced through her neck. Her body sank on its knees and fell onto the street.

"Do not eat," ordered a Jackal. "Save for man's family. But this young one, we eat."

Django became numb to the gore. He stood emotionless. He seemed to accept what they wanted from him. The Jackal that decapitated Yuna raised his axe to slaughter Django.

"Django!" screamed Sam.

Sam quickly pulled out a throwing knife and hurled at the Jackal. The point of the blade landed into the back of the Jackal's skull. The axe clanged to the ground and the Jackal fell on top of Yuna.

"Django, run! Run and don't look back!"

Django snapped out of the trance of death and nodded at Sam. He sprinted out of the alleyway and disappeared.

The Jackals turned towards Sam and rushed him. Sam turned and sped towards the dead end. He was hoping to try to scale the wall with his speed or die trying.

Sam got close to the wall and as he leapt for it, the ground opened, and he fell down a dark chute. The Jackals howled and hollered as Sam slid into the darkness.

Sam slid into a dark chamber. The floor was smooth and made of stone. He couldn't see anything. Sam fumbled around for a few steps in the darkness. He felt a wall. It was cold, smooth, and made of stone. Sam slid his hand along the wall as he carefully walked along the chamber.

Sam stumbled over something dense and smooth. Whatever he tripped on made a rattling noise on the smooth stone floor. Sam got several small cuts and abrasions from the fall. He felt that his lower lip was wet with a little bit of blood. Sam ached as he tried to get up.

Sam used his mind to turn on the light on his cloak. The cloak emanated a dull, orange glow. When Sam realized what he stumbled onto, he lurched back. Bones everywhere. Some animal bones and others were human bones.

He heard metallic growls coming from the other side of the chamber. When Sam looked, his blood ran cold. Five robotic jackals stood there. They slowly headed towards Sam. He saw their blood red, glass eyes and razor-sharp teeth.

"God, please help me!" cried Sam.

The jackals were ready to pounce on Sam. But when they pounced, they died. Sam was bewildered at what just happened. He saw someone standing on the side where the jackals were originally. It was a human jackal. The jackal walked towards Sam. It was a girl around twelve or thirteen. She held a spear with a serrated tip. Her face was painted similar to those who would celebrate Dia De Los Muertos.

"Thank you," said Sam.

The girl nodded in acknowledgment. She motioned Sam to follow her. Sam was reluctant at first but decided to follow. They walked through a narrow tunnel. Fortunately, there were dim lights on the walls of the tunnels for Sam and the girl.

"Where are we going?" asked Sam.

She didn't answer.

Sam wanted to reiterate the question but felt it was wiser not to. They continued through the tunnel. It became serpentine. The tunnel started to have an incline as it continued to contort. The tunnel eventually became straight, but the incline increased.

What a steep climb, Sam thought.

Up ahead, it looked like the night sky. Sam saw the moonlight shining. The girl kept going until she got to the opening of the tunnel. She waited for Sam to come. When he got out, the girl pointed up to go forward.

"You want me to go that way?" asked Sam.

She nodded.

Sam looked around. It seemed they were in the mountains. They were on a path wide enough for cars to go through. As a matter of fact, they were on an old abandoned road. It was a mountain highway at one point. Sam looked behind. He saw the coastal town at the foot of the mountains. He also saw the dilapidated boardwalk. The Nihils were having a bonfire and singing praises to God. And beyond that, Sam saw the beach and the ocean. He saw the clouds speckled with fighter bots patrolling the edges of the Abyss.

Sam turned back to face the road.

"Thank you," said Sam.

The girl was gone. Sam heard a rustle in the trees nearby, but it got fainter as if someone or something was going into the forest. Sam figured it was the girl. In any case, he was thankful and trekked on the lonely road.

33

LONELY ROAD

The crickets chirped. Owls screeched as they carried off mice or hooted in the trees. The moonlight beamed down on Sam. The nocturnal symphony of nature created an abnormal ambience for Sam.

He kept his eyes ahead on the lonely road. It was windy. It was also narrow at some points. Weeds protruded from the cracks in the road.

The walk on this road reminded Sam of what Jesus said about how following Him was a narrow path.

"Enter in by the narrow gate; for wide is the gate and broad is the way that leads to destruction, and many are those who enter in by it. How narrow is the gate, and restricted is the way that leads to life! Few are those who find it."

Sam contemplated Jesus's words as he hiked on the lonely road. This road was like his life. It was not only narrow but also lonely.

As Sam continue to trek along the old highway, thoughts swirled in his mind. Why am I saying I'm here to preach the Gospel but really looking for Beverly? Why I did I come to the Abyss? I feel personally responsible for Yuna's death at the hands of the Jackals. What about Django? Did he escape or die? And for what?! So I can find someone who might not feel the same way? What is wrong with me?

Sam trudged along but as these thoughts weighed him down, his gait slowed. He sank to his knees.

"I'm sorry," he cried upward. "I'm not a worthy servant."

Sam cried till he got too tired to move along. He rested his head against the side of the mountains and fell asleep.

Sam felt a tap on his shoulder. Sam didn't wake up. He felt another tap. Sam woke up. He saw an old man dressed in black clothes.

Behind the man was a truck with its driver's side open. Sam assumed it was his truck.

"You okay there, fella?" asked the man. He had a baritone voice. It was folksy in nature. He had a drawl when he spoke. The man had an accent of a region known as the South when the United States existed.

He had a somewhat muscular built. He was about six feet tall. His hair was silver with some hints of black in it. He had a chiseled jaw and hazel eyes. His demeanor was firm but friendly.

"You want a ride somewhere?"

Sam didn't answer.

"Not much of a talker I suppose. I was driving by and noticed you sleeping on the side of the road and I figured you would like to go someplace more comfortable. Anyway, it's up to you if you want to come. I'll just wait here for a minute or two before I take off."

The man went back into his truck.

Sam sat there. He wasn't sure whether to trust this guy. Sam felt a nudge to get into the truck. But to be safe, Sam discreetly slipped the ring hole of his karambit on his index finger. He softly clenched his fist around the knife. Sam slipped that hand into his cloak. He got up to open the passenger side with the other hand.

The old man nodded as Sam got in. The old man seemed mutually prepared for unknown danger because he had a pistol in a holster on his side. It was a gun you couldn't get legally in mainstream society anymore. Sam glanced at the gun and then looked ahead.

The old man started to drive.

"So, what led you to come out here?" asked the old man.

Sam remained silence.

The old man shrugged.

"Not much of a talker, I see. It's not safe to stay out here, especially at night."

For some reason, the old man's voice sounded familiar to Sam.

"Is there any place you need to go?"

Sam still didn't say a word.

"Look, brother. I'm just trying to help you here."

Sam looked at the man again briefly. He noticed an old Bible seated between him and the old man. He also noticed the old man's jacket that had a UGC emblem on the shoulder. The old man glanced at Sam. He knew what Sam eyed.

"I understand you don't trust the government. I don't either and I work for them. I'm just here to make sure prisoners are well treated. I was hesitant when I took this job, but I felt God called me to do this. After I and other like-minded folks had the government create some monitoring of exile treatment and care, I felt it was hypocritical of me to just sing about it and not do anything else."

Sam turned to old man again. He sounded familiar.

"Aren't you...?"

"You speak. And yes."

This man was a Nouveau Americana singer who would sing about God, Jesus, love, relationships, friendship, indigenous people, the poor, the conditions of prisoners, and, more recently, exiles.

The UGC had some surveillance of this artist but not enough for concern. His criticism of the government and society was mild or very subtle. And the songs about God and Jesus were within the Religious Moderation Act. He didn't compromise but he didn't tell others to come to Jesus. He just sang the songs about the subject without any direct commentary one way or the other.

"You can complain or comment about something," said the old man smiling, "but it doesn't do any good unless you do something, even if it means working within the system."

Sam nodded. He understood where the man was coming from.

"So, young man, where do you want to go?"

"I don't know. I don't know anymore. I don't what I'm doing or why I'm here."

Sam glanced out of his side of the truck. He saw trees, rock, and the side of the mountain. He looked again ahead at the lonely road.

"None of us know really if we were honest with ourselves. All you can do is trust God to lead you, my friend. The Lord Jesus knows the way. Anyway, that's my two cents."

Sam nodded again.

"Yes, that's what I thought. That's why I'm came here."

The old singer turned to Sam. He had a puzzled look.

"Nobody comes here, brother. They are sent here. You mean to tell me you willingly descended into this hell hole?!"

"Yes," Sam replied meekly.

The old man stopped the truck. They both jerked slightly as it halted.

"Well, why would you do a thing like that?!"

Sam told him his reasons. The man pursed his lips as he listened. He nodded along. After Sam finished, he rubbed his chiseled jaw for a bit.

"You know friend," he said slowly. "That's quite a crazy thing to do for love."

Sam moved his head to one side and was bewildered by his remark.

The old man turned his eyes on the road and kept driving. They drove on. Silence took over the cab.

They drove up to a wall. It looked like a checkpoint. The gate at the exit of this checkpoint was made of laser beams. Two armored police officers came towards them. They motioned them to halt. One knocked on the window on the driver's side. The old man lowered his window.

"Whatcha doing here, Old Timer?" asked the officer.

"Just making sure people are well taken care in this hell hole," the old man responded coldly.

Sam could tell the police didn't like the old man, and the feeling was mutual.

"You're not answering the question, Old Man," said the other police officer sharply. "Let's restate the question. What are you doing here?"

The second officer had an icy smile and crazed look. He held his gun, itching to pull the trigger.

The first was more calm and matter of fact. He glanced at the other to ease up.

"Why are you here?" asked the first one.

The old man sighed.

"I came here so you can release him."

"What?!" asked the officers and Sam in unison.

"We can't do that," said the first officers.

"Well, you might have to," the old man replied. "You see this feller isn't a legal exile nor prisoner. He washed up on shore back at the coast. You can't hold him here legally."

The old Nouveau Americana singer went on.

"I suggest you opened that gate," he said as he looked and nodded towards it.

"Come on, Ron," the first officer objected. He shook his head.

"This guy is a prisoner. Don't let your bleeding heart get snowed by it."

"It's not. If this guy telling the truth, then he doesn't belong here. Now you can do this easily or I'll just go above your head."

"Well, good luck," chimed in the second officer. He was referring the possible, looming civil war the world faced and the government's basic inability to do anything in this global ecological crisis.

"Turn this thing around and go or else."

"Or else what," said Ron as he stepped out of the truck.

The second officer raised his gun and aimed it at Ron.

"You guys are bunch of costumed crusaders in the middle of nowhere. You don't have any authority anymore if this government is broken down. You guys get to—."

"Rawwhh!" yelled the second officer as he pulled the trigger. But the gun didn't fire at Ron. It flew out of the officer's hand. The mad dog demur gave away to that of a scared puppy.

Ron held his pistol out. A wisp of smoke came out of the barrel. Ron was known as one of the quickest and best shots in the world. He took down mechanized armor and robots easily in demonstrations. Ron's chiseled face was like stone. His eyes were dark and penetrating.

The first officer drew his weapon.

"You shouldn't have done that."

"What are going to do, kill me?"

Ron didn't turn to face the officer. He kept his eyes on Mr. Trigger Happy.

"Go ahead and try. You don't need this. Go home to your families. I'm not looking to fight with you. The UGC is done and you know that. Now let this guy go or I'll make sure this won't be easy for you two."

The first officer motioned the other officer to picked up his gun and get Sam.

Sam didn't know what to do.

"Search him for a prisoner ID implant."

"All right, you, get out," commanded the second one as manhandled Sam.

"Hey, treat him like a human being not like some rag doll."

"Be quiet, Ron! Don't tell us how to do our job."

The first officer held his gun towards Ron's head. Ron placed his pistol back into his holster.

The second officer scanned Sam thoroughly. This officer forced Sam to strip down naked.

"No ID implant anywhere."

They could all see Sam's naked body. He was curled up on the ground in humiliation. They knew what Sam was.

Ron's blood boiled at what they did to Sam, but he was powerless to stop them.

Sam was in tears. He felt so violated. He turned towards the first officer and Ron. Sam and the first officer's eyes met. There was sadness in the officer's eyes.

The second officer had a sense of sadistic pleasure in reducing Sam to this state.

"So, what are we going to do," he smiled. He licked his lips as he eyed Sam. "It's a..."

"A person," interrupted the first officer. "We are going to let him go."

"Thank you," said Ron meekly.

The first officer didn't acknowledge the gratitude.

"But...," protested the second officer.

"Let him go. He is not legally supposed to be here. So, we're going to let him go."

"What about the knives," insisted the second officers.

"Let him keep them."

"They're knives!"

"I said let him keep them."

The second officer didn't press it further.

The first officer lowered his gun. He went over to Sam. Ron followed him. They picked up Sam's cloak, clothes, and knives.

"Here go ahead and get dressed," the officer said softly to Sam. "You're free to go."

"Thank you," Sam replied. He wiped away the tears.

"We are going to give him some privacy to get dressed."

"What?!" exclaimed the second officer.

"You're sounding like this relic," the second officer said with his hand extended towards Ron. "Besides, stop telling me what to do. Who do you think you are?!"

"You're going to listen," retorted the first officer. Well, because if you don't, this relic and I will make it very difficult for you to be left standing. So, open the damn gate!"

The second officer opened it with his neuroputer. The laser beams dissipated. They turned around so Sam could get dressed.

"I'm done," Sam said weakly.

They turned around.

Sam looked at the first officer and Ron.

"Good luck," said the officer.

"Thank you."

"Godspeed," said Ron as he placed his hands on Sam's shoulder.

"Thank you, brother, for your kindness. May the Lord continue to use you."

Sam looked towards the road and walked out of the Abyss.

34

DAWN OF THE ZEPHYR

It was almost dawn. A zephyr touched Sam's face. Sam was weary from everything. He found a place on the side of the road to lie down. Sam took a smooth stone as a pillow and went to sleep.

The zephyr continued glide against Sam's face as he slept. The zephyr got stronger and it became a chilly wind. It got faster. The wind burned against Sam's cheek. He couldn't sleep anymore. He woke up.

Sam found himself moving in a jeep of some kind. He was lying on the bench seat in the back of the jeep. The jeep had no top. From what he could tell, it was now dawn. Sam felt the ends of soft, long brown hair brushing his cheek on occasion. The hair flowed in the wind. He saw a woman in the driver's seat. Sam sat up on the bench seat. He could see himself in the rear-view mirror. The woman didn't seem aware to be Sam got up.

"Excuse me," asked Sam, "where are we going?"

The woman didn't answer.

"Excuse me."

Still no response.

Sam felt uneasy. The jeep was going at a moderate speed. He discreetly crouched up on the bench seat. Sam was ready to jump. He tried to leap but he couldn't. He fell back onto the seat. Fortunately, his head didn't hit the crossbar or the side.

"You can't jump out. We're cloaked."

Sam recognized the woman's voice, but it sounded slightly cold and hollow.

"Beverly?"

"Hi, Sam."

Beverly glanced over at Sam with a small smile. Beverly turned back to face the road. Sam regained himself to a sitting position.

"Where are we going?"

"I'll explain in a bit."

Strange. Why was Beverly being secretive? Why were they cloaked? Sam wasn't sure what was going on.

"Why are we cloaked then, Bev?"

"To kept us safe, of course."

After Sam seen she wasn't fazed by calling her Bev, he lunged to lock his arm around Beverly's neck. It was an android. He got electrocuted and fell violently back into his seat. Then, darkness.

Sam woke up. He doesn't know what happened, but he is sure he had been knocked out several times.

Sam thought, I really need to stop doing this. As usual, Sam noticed he was lying in a bed. But this time, he sensed it was different. He couldn't move. Sam struggled to get up but not one fiber of muscle could budge. Was he paralyzed now? Sam focused on what he could do—use his eyes.

He saw he was in a room with walls that seemed to be padded or insulated with some kind of material. On the left side of the room, Sam saw another bed. There was a small circular window above him on the wall. On the ceiling was a concave translucent dome with a plus frame running across it, the dome seemed to be split into four panels. Sam saw a door ahead of him that was closed. For what seemed like eons, Sam lied there unable to move. Sam drifted back off to sleep.

"Sam....Sam."

Sam felt someone shake him. Sam woke up. Beverly was over him.

"Beverly?!"

Sam was able to sit up this time. Sam looked at Beverly. Beverly looked at Sam. Sam then remembered what happened before he blacked out. He became apprehensive towards Beverly.

"Sam."

He was silent.

"Sam."

He didn't respond. Sam looked in vain for his karambit.

"Sam," Beverly said as she gently placed her hand on Sam's arm. He winced. "We don't have time. We must go."

"Go?" asked Sam. "Where are we going?" His voice kept a tone of mistrust like his body language.

"No time to explain, Sam. There's much to do but not much time."

"What if I don't want to go."

"Sam, this isn't an option."

Her gentle touch became a firm grip. It felt like a vice grip. Sam couldn't get out of it.

"It's time."

"To do what?"

"It's time to see and feel the dawn of the zephyr."

35

FEEL THE ZEPHYR

Beverly led Sam into an enormous chamber. It was like they were inside a giant sphere. He couldn't tell whether inside was made of metal, glass, or something else. The inside was multi-hued like that of a rainbow.

Sam felt very insignificant because of the chamber's size. Though the chamber and the opening were big enough to attempt an escape, he felt it was unwise to do so.

"Where the hell are we?"

Sam's question reverberated throughout the sphere.

"You will know all things. Just wait."

Beverly's voice, or the android of her—he still wasn't sure—echoed too. It was still cold and slightly metallic.

They stood there for a bit. Then Beverly raised both her arms in the air.

"It's time!"

Sam felt something like a gentle breeze. It was similar to the zephyr he felt before he was captured.

The wind howled inside the chamber. But this wind felt unlike anything Sam felt before. It tingled his skin like that of mild electric shocks.

Sam again couldn't move. He saw what looked like sparks or electric discharge covering his body. Fear and euphoria enveloped Sam. He never felt anything like it.

"Don't fight it, Sam! Be one with the zephyr. Let yourself ascend into infinity!"

She still had her hands raised. Sparks emanated from them and soon filled the entire chamber.

Sam began to see what look like apparitions of people. They flicked in and out inside the chamber. Sam heard what was like a waterfall of voices. Then followed by a river of music and other sounds.

Sam was overwhelmed by everything. He recognized all this as soul data. But why all here? Then, Sam felt like he was about go into a seizure.

"Don't resist, Sam. Become one with the zephyr. Become one with all!"

Beverly suddenly flashed before him. She placed her hand on his cheek. She gently glided her fingers. Sam closed his eyes and felt enraptured by her sensuality.

"Become one with me," she whispered in his ear.

Beverly flashed back to her original spot. Sam opened his eyes. He smiled as she stood there.

Beverly yelled, "this is our destiny!"

"What is..."

"To become one. To reach our zenith. To become the Universe. To become god!"

"That's blasphemy!" yelled Sam.

He finally noticed a circular patch on the side of her shoulder that had the seven-headed, ten-horned dragon symbol of Dragon Corp. Was this really Beverly or a cheap imitation?

"Is it," she asked in a mischievous manner. She smiled while biting her lip.

Beverly vanished and reappeared before Sam. She touched his face again softly. Sam closed his eyes but this time he tried to pull back.

"Or is it the truth, blasphemer?"

Beverly's voice changed to that of a man. Sam opened his eyes. He gasped in horror. Then, he felt a grip by his neck and lifted up by his throat.

"Eron!"

"In the flesh...for now. Uh-ha, ha...Uh-ha-ha! Ha, ha, ha, ha!"

Eron released his grip. Sam fell.

"Don't your Scriptures say, 'you are gods'. Even Jesus restated this in front of *His* opponents. And, as *He* said, 'Scripture cannot be broken.' "

Eron smiled. He then turned around and look around to admire his chamber.

"Ah, Jesus, *He* was a visionary for saying such as a thing. I did admire *Him*. Too bad *His* followers distorted *His* teachings. You know. I was a Christian once myself. But now, I realized the truths of our destiny."

"What did you do to Beverly?" asked Sam as he struggled to get up. The lightning-like currents that enveloped his body served as shackles now.

"What I did to do? Why don't you ask yourself!"
Sam was puzzled.
Eron shook his head.
"You don't get it do you? Here let me illustrate this for you, Sam."
Then, something that looked like haze materialized above. In the midst of the haze, there appeared a city street. It looked like it was nighttime. Sam saw a woman stepping out a building that looked like a church. Sam recognized the woman. It was Beverly!
Then, Sam realized what was going to happen, the horror that ensued.
"Noooo!"
Sam closed his eyes. He slumped back to the floor.
"Yes, Sam. You killed her! You killed her because she was a Christian. Now out of your guilty conscience you become one yourself."
Sam raised his head at Eron in defiance.
"You're a liar, Eron! She's alive! I sat with her. I ate with her. She let me stay with her when I had no home. She taught me the Scriptures and the ways of my Lord. She showed me her scar and even forgave me. She was even thankful I did that."
Eron grinned.
"Are you finished, Sam?"
Sam did not respond.
"You see, Sam, what you just described is a miracle. It's a miracle that doesn't require God."

36

FOLLOW THE WIND

"What?!" Sam exclaimed. "That doesn't make any sense, Eron!"

Eron shook his head and smiled.

"Oh, but it does, Sam, if you're willing to hear and willing to see."

Sam said nothing. He felt the virtual shackles wrapped around him got heavier.

Beverly materialized before their eyes.

"Beverly!" exclaimed Sam.

"Sam," she replied in her normal tone. "What happened to you?"

She ran over to Sam to try to free him.

"Beverly, don't!"

Her hand went through the electrical shackles and through Sam's body. Sam felt nothing. Beverly pulled back in amazement. She tried again but the same thing happened.

"Ha, ha, Beverly, you want to know why you can't touch Sam," said Eron in glee.

"Why?"

"It's because you're dead!"

"Liar," retorted Beverly.

"No, it's true. Your soulmate here killed you."

"I don't believe you."

"Silly Ms. Bonnevara, ye of little faith!"

Eron with his neuroputer had images emanating from his eyes before them. It showed what happened after Sam sliced her neck. She bled profusely from the deep wound. Beverly also cracked her head from the fall, so she bled from the back of head as well. Patrol bots saw her lying on the sidewalk and alerted a nearby ambulance. The images flickered to her on an operating table. The doctors and nurses shook their heads as they walked away from the table. Beverly lied there motionless. Then, a doctor scanned for her dossier and typed "Decreased". The images vanished.

"I don't understand..."

Beverly shook her hand.

"No, this is a lie. I can't be dead."

"Oh...but you are."

"Stop it! I can't be. I have been living since that night. I have come into a new life in Jesus Christ. And part of that new life was eating, talking, and spending time with Sam. I don't know what you're trying to pull here. This...."

Eron burst into raucous laughter. Sam and Beverly looked at each other with fear and uncertainty. What was this madman babbling and laughing about? Eron calmed down. He nodded his head.

"Of course, you experienced those things, Beverly. But Christ didn't give you a new life, I did. You see, Beverly, you have been resurrected as a living soul data. You are the first and only at this time."

Beverly and Sam didn't know what to say.

"You see," said Eron as he paced around the chamber. "Rather than waiting or hoping there's an afterlife, reincarnation, or a resurrection from a god or a cosmic force, I was able to spearhead the concept and technology to do this now. Why settle for an ordinary soul data that is just a glorified recording of the deceased?"

Eron arms spanned out. His eyes grew wide and his voice increased in volume from enthusiasm.

"This," he pointed at Beverly, "is the end of faith and empty hope. And you my dear have reaffirmed it! You are the end of death and suffering! You should feel honored."

"What I feel is disgust," protested Beverly. "You dare to play God by using me as a guinea pig. I should have died a long time ago."

"Then you wouldn't have met Sam," retorted Eron. "You wouldn't have introduced him, her, or it to the Gospel of Jesus Christ. You did well, my dear! Though you died, you were alive. I even saw you use the fighting abilities that I programmed you with to protect Sam from those Nihils. I know how much you love him. I wanted to give you an edge to your personality. I saw it all! Your mystery woman in black, Sam!"

Beverly turned to Sam and nodded. But she hated what she was: a digital shadow of her former self.

Sam mustered enough to stand up.

"What's your endgame, Eron," Sam demanded.

"My endgame, Sam?! It's more like a new beginning for humanity. I'm doing everything I can preserve our species and help it excel. It needs to take its rightful place as heirs to the Kingdom of the Universe. The only way for that to happen is if we possess power and immortality."

Sam was befuddled by his rhetoric. Surprisingly, he grew stronger or he finally adjusted to these bizarre shackles. He noticed Beverly's soul data slouching on the ground in despair. It didn't matter what she was. Sam considered her to be just...Beverly.

"Beverly," said Sam.

She didn't respond.

"Beverly."

She slowly looked up. Her face was saddened.

"Listen, it doesn't matter whether you're physically alive or not, you're still the Beverly I know. I don't know how or what happened, but I know you're alive in Christ, soul data or not. We know the God we follow is greater than this madman's scheme. He doesn't get it. We trust that God's love and grace is bigger than anything we can imagine. You belong to Christ and you're more alive than ever. And Beverly, I also..."

Eron shook his head. He chuckled.

"Why are you holding on to a dead Jewish guy. Let me show you something. This may change your minds."

He snapped his fingers and suddenly the chains disappeared from Sam. His body felt different somehow. He felt more muscular and the occasional sickly feeling was non-existent. And he saw Beverly as before, she had her body back. Beverly looked down and grasped her arms. She looked up at Sam.

The chamber was also transformed into what seemed to be a side of a small mountain, where there was a forest surrounding a mountain. They saw a shimmering big, beautiful, blue lake. They felt a cool zephyr coming through and gliding across their faces.

"What's going on," demanded Sam.

"You are in what you and Beverly would call Paradise. I know, I heard it all."

Sam and Beverly once talked about an ideal place. This place was a yearning they had where it was a realm where this was absolute peace, beauty, and freedom. If such a place that came close existed, they said they would go to that place.

Beverly went towards Sam. She clasped onto to his left hand.

"Isn't that nice," chuckled Eron, "a man and a woman who love each other. That's precious. Sam, examine yourself, my friend."

Sam looked at his body. It was of a slight muscular build. The skin tone was a slightly silver. He felt his face. It was different. And, finally, he felt down below, it was different too.

"Yes, you're a complete man. You can choose a woman body or remain as you are but better. It doesn't matter. The point is physical deformities and mental ones will be irrelevant now."

"How?" asked Beverly.

"When you connect your soul data to this neuronetwork that I'm showing before you, you can be in your ideal world and your ideal body. No more suffering and pain. You just will it and it will happen. The stupid laws about Undesirables from the United Gaia Council are irrelevant. As a matter of fact, we don't need them anymore. I'm glad this disaster happened. People will be open to this new way when the civil war intensifies."

"So, what does this have to do with us? And how do you know the civil war will continue," Sam pressed.

Eron grinned.

"You will bring this message of hope. If they accept, then you will shower them with specially designed neurons that will connect them to the neuronetwork. I will modify your body so you can do this."

A small bag appeared in the palm of Eron's hand. Inside the bag looked like small speckles of gold.

"Think of it like a baptism, if you will. We can rebuild our species out of the ashes of this dead world. Our ultimate goal is to ascend as our rightful rulers of this Universe."

Sam was still skeptical of this proposal.

"Why us?" asked Sam. "What makes you think people are going let themselves get showered with this stuff? And who says we are the rightful rulers of the Universe. Where do you get this from?"

The small bag vanished from Eron's hand. Beverly and Sam could hear the birds chirping and a river roaring in their paradise.

"It's because I know you two have the ability to persuade and teach others. I have seen you do this with your Jesus. Why not use these abilities to bring this better message of hope? Of hope we can have now. God and death and suffering become irrelevant. We can create our own realities. And we are not going to force people to join. That's the damn State who practices this. We'll just nudge them in the direction we want them to, so they can unite with us."

"How are you going to pull that off," Beverly chimed in. "This is looney."

"Ohh, it will be looney if they resist. We will fund weapons, bandages, and propaganda to the UGC and the secessionists. We will make sure this civil war is the worst conflict humankind has ever seen. It will be a long-term plan and it may take decades, but the option will be clear: have eternal life and a chance to ascend into the stars or perish in your folly."

Sam shook his head.

"Sorry, I'm not buying it, Eron. I'm committed to Christ."

Eron shook his head in response.

"And what has Jesus has done for you, huh! All you have gotten is suffering and pain. It's not worth it. Yes, *He* told you to deny yourself and take up your cross and follow *Him*. I know the cost to follow Jesus but is it worth it Sam?! Is it?! I know I used to be like you at one point. Join us or else."

"Or else, what?!"

"This."

Eron snapped his finger. The pristine paradise vanished. Beverly's body reverted back to soul data. And Sam became himself again. Then, what looked like a barbed wire of electrical current wrapped around Beverly.

"Ahhhh!" Beverly screamed.

"Beverly!"

Sam tried to free her, but it was no use. He got shocked and fell back. But fortunately, Sam still had a karambit. He drew with intense speed and pounced on Eron with intense force. He sliced Eron's side. To his surprise, it was sparks that emit, not blood that flowed.

"An android! Let her go, Bastard!"

"Oh, I will, Sam. Into oblivion!"

Eron pushed Sam off. He punched Sam. The karambit flew from his hand. Eron punched a few more times. The blows felt like a hammer to Sam. Sam's face was blooded. Eron gripped Sam's neck and lifted him up.

"I tried to be reasonable, but you won't return the reason. You could have had it all. Eternal life. Paradise. A perfect body. The girl. But now, you'll get nothing. Go into oblivion with your precious Beverly! Rawwr!!"

"Noooo!" screamed a woman.

A dagger sailed through the air and landed smack into Eron's left eye. He dropped Sam. He roared. Eron pulled the dagger out and started laughing.

It was Elmira. She drew a tomahawk from underneath her coat and pounced onto Eron. Elmira hacked and slashed ferociously. It seemed Eron was outmatched. Sparks emitted from his body from the gashes.

"You fool! You can't kill me."

"I may not be able to kill you, but I'll save my daughter and Sam and shut you down."

Then, Eron's arm morphed into a chain gun. He pelted Elmira's body a few times. Despite the shots, Elmira didn't falter in her attack. She kept up her savage onslaught on Eron. She grappled Eron and severed the connections on the chain gun. The chain gun fell to the ground.

Eron roared again. His arm morphed again into what looked a sword. Eron grabbed Elmira and punctured her body. The sword went through her body. At that moment, Eron spewed the same type of sparkling dust over Elmira's face that he offered Sam to use on others.

He retracted the sword. His arm became an arm again. Sam scurried over to Elmira.

"Noooo!" he screamed.

"Mom!" cried Beverly. She desperately tried to clutch her mother, but it was a vain attempt.

Sam cradled Elmira.

"No greater love than this: which is to lay down for your life for your friends," she said weakly.

Elmira stealthily gave something to Sam. Elmira met God. Sam wept.

"Don't weep, Sam, she can be brought back," Eron reassured.

"You're a sick man, Eron!"

"Sam, people will try to stop and destroy what they don't understand. That's been the case with all religions. But this time, this is a real chance for actual salvation for humanity. And not only salvation but thriving as a species and conquering the stars. It is our destiny, Sam."

Beverly couldn't speak. All she could think about was her mother.

"So, what's it going to be, Sam? Will you embrace the future and Elmira and Beverly will live again? Or will you hold onto to the past—and you know what happens if you do that. The choice is yours."

Sam looked at Beverly and looked down at Elmira. He looked at Eron and then Beverly again. Beverly gave him a weak shake of disapproval. Sam bowed and closed his eyes.

"All right, let's embrace...the future."

Eron smiled.

"Welcome home, son. Now it's your time to shine brighter than your Lord!"

37

AND SO IT BEGINS

Sam trekked through a mountainous area. Sam was fitted with some kind of small cannon on his arm that would emit the dust of immortality, as Eron called it, on those who would accept. Beverly was with him but in an android body. She didn't speak to Sam since they left Eron. She was compelled to go with Sam as a reminder to not deviate from the message. If he did, then Beverly and Elmira would be deleted. Eron made sure by having a link connected to Beverly's soul data to enforce protocol.

"Beverly," Sam called once again. But she ignored him. She wouldn't even walk close by. She just walked close enough to keep an eye on Sam. Then, they saw in a valley about a couple of miles below. They heard shouts, machines clashing, and gunfire below. It was the UGC police, who now turned into soldiers, versus the separatist confederation forces. Sam zoomed on his binoculars to get a better view of them. The battle was intense. Many were injured or killed on each side. Sam noticed that both sides used weapons and equipment from Dragon Corp. It was strange to see a myriad of the same scarlet seven-headed, ten-horned dragons clashing with each other.

Sam rested the binoculars around his neck and turned around to Beverly.

"And so, it begins...Beverly. Let's go down there."

"Okay," she said tersely.

They trekked down the mountain until they got to the foot of it. The battle got louder and more intense as they move closer. There was a barrier of trees that separated them from the battle. Sam put his hand in his coat pocket. He clutched the small note Elmira gave him before she died. Sam pulled it out to read the note.

Beverly looked puzzled at what he was doing. So was Eron.

Then, Sam felt a familiar and warm hand on his shoulder.

"Sam."

Sam turned around.

"Lord!"

Sam knelt before Jesus.

Beverly didn't see who or what Sam was knelling at.

"No one, having put his hand to the plow, and looking back, is fit for God's Kingdom."

Jesus vanished.

Sam rose to his feet.

Beverly just stood there.

"What was that about, Sam?"

"I would like to know," said Eron as he observed them. They didn't hear him.

"Beverly, 'No one, having put his hand to the plow, and looking back, is fit for God's Kingdom'."

"What? I don't understand."

"No one, having put his hand to the plow, and looking back, is fit for God's Kingdom. I'm sorry Beverly, but I need to do this."

He clutched her wrist. She tried to pull back but couldn't. Sam kissed Beverly. At first, she resisted but kissed him willingly. Eron was puzzled again. Her body lit up and emitted a small blue light around her. Sam let go.

"I love you, Beverly. I will always love you. But I love our Lord more."

Sam wiped the tears from his face and rushed through the barrier of trees into the thicket of battle. He left Beverly behind.

Sam stood between the opposing force. Strange enough, they stopped when they saw him. Sam threw the arm cannon down. He raised both his arms.

"I have a message for all of you! God loves you. He loves all of us. He showed us by sending His Son, so we may not perish but have everlasting life. His Son showed us how to be towards each other and towards God. His Son's name is Jesus Christ. He is the King of the Universe and asking for us to submit to join His Kingdom. His Kingdom is full of love, grace, justice, and truth. His yoke is easy, and His burden is light. Lay your weapons down and follow Him!"